Brad murmured tauntingly.

So, Sabrina noted, the battle of wills had begun. Which would it be? A verbal shoot-out at high noon or visual daggers at dawn?

Staring into Brad's brown eyes, she recognized the boldly provocative look he was giving her. But he'd definitely grown up. At least physically.

"Enjoying the view?" Brad inquired.

Two could play mind games, Sabrina decided. "Actually, I was trying to remember where I'd seen you before."

"Do a lot of guys call you Golden Girl?" he demanded.

"No, thank goodness."

"Coming back to you now, is it?"

She nodded. "You know, I almost didn't recognize you without your black T-shirt and a cigarette dangling out of your mouth," she noted.

"I gave up smoking. Bad for your sex life."

"A fascinating discovery, I'm sure. But I'm not here to discuss your sex life...."

Dear Reader,

Welcome to Silhouette Desire! If this is your first Desire novel, I hope it will be the first of many. If you're a regular reader, you already know that you're in for a treat.

Every Silhouette Desire book contains a romance to remember. These stories can be dramatic or humorous... topical or traditional. Each and every one is a love story that is guaranteed to sweep you into a world of passion. The heroines are women with hopes and fears just like yours. And the heroes—watch out! You won't want to read about just one. It will take all six of these strong men to keep you satisfied.

Next month, look for a special treat... six tantalizing heroes you'll want to get to know—and love—in *Men of the World*. These sinfully sexy men are from six different and romantic countries. Each book has the portrait of your hero on the cover, so you won't be able to miss this handsome lineup. Our featured authors are some of the finest: BJ James, Barbara Faith, Jennifer Greene, Lucy Gordon, Kathleen Korbel and Linda Lael Miller. *Men of the World*—don't miss them.

And don't miss September's *Man of the Month* book, *Lone Wolf* by Annette Broadrick. It sizzles!

Happy reading,

Lucia Macro
Senior Editor

CATHIE LINZ
SMOOTH SAILING

Published by Silhouette Books New York

America's Publisher of Contemporary Romance

SILHOUETTE BOOKS
300 East 42nd St., New York, N.Y. 10017

SMOOTH SAILING

Copyright © 1991 by Cathie L. Baumgardner

All rights reserved. Except for use in any review, the reproduction or utilization of this work in whole or in part in any form by any electronic, mechanical or other means, now known or hereafter invented, including xerography, photocopying and recording, or in any information storage or retrieval system, is forbidden without the permission of the publisher, Silhouette Books, 300 E. 42nd St., New York, N.Y. 10017

ISBN: 0-373-05665-6

First Silhouette Books printing September 1991

All the characters in this book have no existence outside the imagination of the author and have no relation whatsoever to anyone bearing the same name or names. They are not even distantly inspired by any individual known or unknown to the author, and all incidents are pure invention.

® and ™: Trademarks used with authorization. Trademarks indicated with ® are registered in the United Patent and Trademark Office, the Canada Trade Mark Office and in other countries.

Printed in the U.S.A.

Books by Cathie Linz

Silhouette Desire

Change of Heart #408
A Friend in Need #443
As Good as Gold #484
Adam's Way #519
Smiles #575
Handyman #616
Smooth Sailing #665

CATHIE LINZ

was in her mid-twenties when she left her career in a university law library to become a full-time writer of contemporary romance fiction. Since then, this Chicago author has had almost twenty books published. She enjoys hearing from readers and has received fan mail from as far away as Nigeria!

An avid world traveler, Cathie often uses humorous mishaps from her own trips as inspiration for her stories. Still, she's always glad to get back home to her two cats, her trusty word processor and her hidden cache of Oreo cookies!

For the wild ones—my two cats—
and for those who appreciate feline antics.

One

"I'm telling you—the man hates me!" Sabrina Stewart informed her boss. "If Brad Romanovski finds out I'm working for your video production company, he'll never do business with you! Believe me, I'm not the right person for *this* assignment."

Sabrina paused, well aware of the surprised look Eliot Wainscott was giving her. Not once in the few months she'd been working with him here in Newport had she ever displayed the slightest tendency toward agitation or exaggeration. Sabrina prided herself on being able to remain cool, calm and collected—regardless of the circumstances.

But the possibility of having to do business with Brad Romanovski was enough to push her internal panic button, a button she thought she'd deactivated years ago.

"I've never seen you this upset," Eliot noted. "Don't you think you might be overstating the situation a little?"

Looking Eliot in the eye, Sabrina said, "Do you really think I'm the type who panics easily?"

"Quite the opposite. Nothing ever seems to faze you," Eliot admitted.

"Then trust me." Her voice was more composed now, though no less vehement. "This would *not* work out. For the good of the company, it would be better if someone else handles this one."

The fact that Sabrina had known Eliot for years before she started to work for him made it easier for her to be frank. Eliot had been good to her. She didn't want to cause him or Memories, the video production company he owned, any trouble. "Trouble," however, was Brad Romanovski's middle name! "I'd even be willing to take on the Newman family, all one hundred of them, and their reunion," she offered. "Anything rather than Brad Romanovski."

"What makes you think that Romanovski hates you?" Eliot countered.

"Past experience," Sabrina stated darkly.

"I had no idea you two had a history," Eliot said.

"We don't," she denied. "Not really."

"What would you call it then?"

"A mutual dislike that dates back to my teenage days. From the time I was fifteen until I was twenty, Brad Romanovski delighted in making my life miserable every summer. He used to get a kick out of humiliating me in public. He'd call me Golden Girl and make fun of me—of the way I walked, of my Boston accent. He turned up everywhere, never joining in, just standing there, leaning against his souped-up car, whistling, cat-calling and generally making a nuisance of himself."

"Sounds like he liked you."

Sabrina looked at Eliot as if he'd taken leave of his senses. "No way! I'm telling you, he hated me. Besides, he always had a sultry, dark-haired girlfriend with him. A different one each year, but they always looked like they'd been around the block a few times." They'd also worn the skimpiest halter tops Sabrina had ever seen, but she omitted adding that fact. "Brad detested me because I was rich. That, or he hated blondes." She shrugged. "I don't know what his problem was. Actually, I'm surprised he's still here in Newport. I got the impression from his attitude that he wasn't particularly enamored with this area. I would have thought he'd have left Rhode Island far behind him now."

"He's not only stayed in Newport, he's doing quite well here," Eliot stated. "His services are very much in demand. He started his own business, Neptune Security, a few years ago. The timing was perfect. With boat robberies on the rise, more and more yacht owners are installing increasingly complicated security systems. I hear he has more business than he knows what to do with."

"I imagine Brad would be good at installing security systems. He's probably gotten around a few of them in his day," Sabrina murmured to herself.

Hearing her, Eliot shook a reprimanding finger at her. "Is that any way to talk about a prospective client?"

Sabrina tried to look contrite but failed. "I can't help it. The man is a nemesis from my past. I'm telling you, we don't get along. It would be disastrous to send me out on this job. Disastrous!"

"But, Brad, all the best families here in Newport are doing it!" Helen told her brother as they sat on the couch in his office.

"I don't care if they're doing the lambada naked on Ocean Drive," Brad Romanovski retorted. "You of all people should know that I don't give a tinker's damn what Rhode Island's best families are doing."

"They do come up with some good ideas every once in a while, you know."

"Yeah," he agreed laconically. "Once every hundred years or so."

"Come on." Helen swatted him with a rolled up magazine. "All I'm saying is that a video compilation of our family's history would be a great gift for Grandmother and Granddad's anniversary. At least talk to the representative from the production company before you make up your mind. Ms. Stewart's coming here to your office at four."

"Ms. Stewart?" Brad repeated, reminding himself that there were millions of Stewarts in the world. It was a very common name. It just had a lot of very *un*common memories for him. He was simply glad that his sister didn't know anything about his obsession during that period in his life. No one in his family did.

It wasn't something he'd bragged about—being hung up on a ritzy blonde with frosty blue eyes. As a cocky teenager he'd been too "cool" to be hung up on anyone. At least that's what he'd taken great pains in those days to make everyone think. Including his little sister, Helen.

"Actually, she told me to call her Sabrina," Helen was saying, "but knowing your reputation with women I think it would be best if you kept things on a business level and called her Ms. Stewart." Noticing the hard-jawed look on her brother's face, Helen sighed. "Now what's wrong?"

It *was* her! Sabrina Stewart. Back in Newport. The news took Brad completely by surprise. He hadn't felt this way since a boom had once caught him on the side of the head.

Then he'd seen stars.

Now he saw a chance to get even.

A phone call interrupted Sabrina's discussion with Eliot. After hanging up, he gave her a knowing look. "Brad Romanovski hates you, hmm?"

Sabrina nodded. "That's right."

"If that's the case, then why did Brad just have his secretary call to confirm your appointment for this afternoon—making it quite clear that he wanted you to show up. No last-minute replacements, is what he said."

"There." Sabrina emphatically tapped the tip of her index finger on the corner of Eliot's desk, nearly bending over the nail it had taken her weeks to grow. "You see? He's setting me up."

"Paranoid, aren't you?"

"Where Brad Romanovski is concerned, you bet I am."

"You're both adults now. It's time you buried the hatchet. And not in each other's heads," Eliot added, noting the look in Sabrina's eyes. "It's time to let bygones be bygones."

"Live and let live, hmm?"

Eliot nodded.

Sabrina sighed. She could tell from his expression that Eliot wasn't going to change his mind. "Maybe you're right. Maybe I am overreacting. As you pointed out, Brad and I are adults now. What happened between us did take place eight years ago. I haven't seen him since then. No doubt we've both changed a lot over the years. If we have any differences, I'm sure we can set them aside." Sabrina was sure *she* could set them aside, but how Brad would react was anyone's guess. Unpredictability had always been his specialty. "Whatever happens, I'm not going to let him get to me," she stated firmly.

"That's the spirit!" Eliot congratulated her.

Helen had barely left his office when Brad began mentally rubbing his hands together with glee. Sabrina Stewart—the Golden Girl. Coming to see him. He couldn't believe it.

As a teenager Brad had dreamed of the day when Sabrina would come to him. He'd conjured up scenarios where she'd run to him and beg for his help or plead for his attention. He'd visualized himself kissing her senseless and then coldheartedly turning her away—thereby punishing her for the way she'd looked right through him when he'd spent his summers eating his heart out for her.

With her blue eyes and long golden hair, Sabrina Stewart had been the star of a number of his steamiest teenage fantasies. She was, as one of his fishing buddies had put it, "The one that got away."

She'd had a body to die for. He could still remember how the sexy sway of her walk had made his mouth go dry. But she'd never even given him the time of day.

She'd only come to Newport for the summers, which she spent with her own kind—the privileged ones, the wealthy ones. They'd cruise Thames Street in their vanity-plated Corvette convertibles while he was working like a slave at Murray's Garage. Sabrina and her crowd had had no time for a guy who got his hands dirty. They'd laughed at him, ridiculing his foreign-sounding name, mocking his working-class background.

Now here Sabrina Stewart was—back in Newport, after all this time. And due to stroll into his office in two hours. Brad could hardly wait.

"He who laughs last..." he muttered.

By the time Sabrina entered the offices of Neptune Security, she had herself completely under control once more. Eliot was right, it really wasn't like her to get so upset. After all, since her return to Newport a few months ago, she'd dealt with a number of on-the-job crises without batting an eye: from the Ferguson twins' New-Age wedding to the taping of Mrs. Simpson's pedigree Afghan giving birth to puppies.

Sabrina smoothed an imaginary wrinkle from the skirt of her navy-blue dress. She'd been sitting, cooling her heels, in Brad Romanovski's outer office for almost fifteen minutes now. If this was his way of waging a battle of wills, he had a lot to learn. He wasn't going to throw her off balance. She'd changed from the vulnerable teenager she'd once been. Or so she kept reminding herself.

"Mr. Romanovski will see you now," his secretary finally informed her. "You can go on in."

"Thank you," Sabrina said. The woman reminded her of all those dark-haired sirens Brad had gone with during his teenage years. Obviously the man still had a thing for sultry brunettes. Which is irrelevant, she silently reprimanded herself. Keep your focus on business. Brad is merely another potential client. Nothing more than that. Don't let yourself get distracted. Don't let *him* distract you.

She placed a steady hand on the doorknob. Ready or not, here I come, Mr. Romanovski!

But when Sabrina sailed into Brad's office, the chair behind his desk was empty. A quick glance around the room failed to locate him. Was this some kind of trick? she wondered with irritation. If so, it would appear that Brad Romanovski hadn't grown up much after all.

While standing there, pondering her next move, Sabrina couldn't help noticing the stuffed fish on the wall. It was hard to miss—since it was staring right at her with unmistakable malevolence. In fact, there was something about it, a certain steeliness in its single eye, that was eerily familiar. It reminded her of someone. Brad, perhaps? A bit disconcerted, she hurriedly looked away.

Now what? Should I stay or leave? Sabrina was in the midst of reviewing her options, when the door slammed behind her.

"Having second thoughts, Golden Girl?" Brad murmured tauntingly.

Two

So, Sabrina noted with rueful resignation, the battle of wills has begun. She'd have to choose her weapons carefully. Which would it be? A verbal shoot-out at high noon or visual daggers at dawn? She opted for words.

"A little old to be playing hide-and-seek, aren't you?" she stated calmly.

"Some games get better as you get older," Brad returned.

"I wouldn't know."

"That doesn't surprise me," he drawled.

Staring into Brad's brown eyes, Sabrina recognized the boldly provocative look he was giving her. She'd been mistaken. His gaze bore no resemblance to that of the stuffed fish on the wall. None at all.

And he'd definitely grown up. At least physically.

Brad had always been tall, but he seemed more hardened now than he'd been the last time she'd seen him. That made sense. Then he'd only been two or three years over the legal drinking age of twenty-one. Now he was a man of... She did some hasty mental arithmetic. He must be about thirty-two. Which would explain the almost intangible air of strength and authority he now possessed—this despite the fact that he was dressed casually in black slacks and a short-sleeved navy-blue shirt. No business suit for him.

Yes, Sabrina had to admit, Brad had definitely matured well—although the gleam in his eyes made her wonder if she'd used the term *mature* correctly. Because it was clear to her that the trouble-making rebel she'd known as a teenager hadn't transformed himself completely. That part of his nature was still a force to be reckoned with—she could see it in the cocky confidence of his smile.

"Enjoying the view?" he inquired.

Two could play mind games, she decided. "Actually I was trying to remember where I'd seen you before," she returned without missing a beat. His frown was worth the momentary guilt she felt at fibbing.

"A lot of guys call you Golden Girl?" he demanded.

"No, thank goodness."

"Coming back to you now, is it?"

She nodded. "You know, I almost didn't recognize you without your black T-shirt and a cigarette dangling out of your mouth," she noted.

"I gave up smoking. Bad for your sex life."

"A fascinating discovery, I'm sure. But I'm not here to discuss your sex life..."

"Too bad," he inserted.

"I'm here to discuss a video compilation of your family's history, Mr. Romanovski," she went on without missing a beat. "I understand, according to your sister, that this video would be for your grandparents' fiftieth wedding anniversary? Is that correct?"

"My name's Brad."

Since his answer had nothing to do with her question, she eyed him cautiously, wondering what he was up to now. "That's right. So?"

"So use it. Not Mr. Romanovski. My dad's called Mr. Romanovski. I'm called Brad."

When you're not being called something worse, Sabrina thought to herself. "Well, Brad, as I was saying..."

He waved his hand impatiently while belatedly answering her original question. "Yeah, this tape thing would be for my grandparents' anniversary. You don't have to recite the entire spiel again. I'm not stupid."

No, just obnoxious. Sabrina stopped herself from voicing the words aloud, but only just. It required biting her tongue—literally. She then took a deep breath and reminded herself that Brad was a potential client and as such should be treated with courtesy.

"Did you have any questions, Brad?"

Brad had plenty. What had Sabrina been doing for the past eight years? Why was she back in Newport now after all this time? Did she like long, slow kisses or fast, hot ones? Why couldn't she have gained thirty pounds and looked like a dumpster?

Nothing was supposed to be as good as you remembered. Why did Sabrina have to be the exception?

She was still the epitome of class and cool sophistication. Even more aggravating, she was still sexy as hell. Brad thought that the least she could have done was to cut her glorious mane of silky blond hair into one of those short, spiky masculine hairdos that seemed to be the rage now. But no, she'd kept her hair long. Today the silky strands were held away from her face by a large gold barrette.

He'd forgotten how big her blue eyes were. And how intense. They were the color of the ocean he loved so much.

"Perhaps I should rephrase that last question, since you appear to be having trouble with it," she said with a kindness only slightly laced with mockery. "Was there something else I can tell you about our video production company?"

"You own it?"

His curt question startled her. "Me? No. I work for Memories."

"Why?"

"Because I want to."

"Do you always do what you want?" he countered.

"I don't see that this line of questioning is really relevant. If we could leave our personalities behind and focus on the matter at hand..." Her voice trailed off as he moved toward her. Now what was he up to?

"Certainly." Brad surprised her by strolling past her to his desk where he dropped into his chair. "Sit. No need to stand on formality here."

She lowered herself onto the visitor's chair as if sitting on pins and needles. Seeing his amused look, she deliberately forced herself to relax, and even crossed her legs—daintily at the ankle—before tucking them under the chair the way her grandmother had taught her. "Did your sister tell you anything about the kind of videotaping services we provide?" Sabrina said briskly.

"She said all the best families in Newport are using your services."

Sabrina didn't like the way he'd worded that. She suspiciously checked his face for any sign of derision, but his expression was as innocent as a newborn baby's—no mean feat for a bad boy like Brad.

"The company has been doing very well," she stated. "We videotape weddings, bar mitzvahs, birthdays and other special occasions. The family chronicles, which is what we call the family history compilations, have been extremely popular. Basically what we do is make use of any old home movies you might have, plus old photographs and slides, and put together a storyboard of your family history. We transfer the old eight-millimeter movies onto video tape, and make some sense out of them. By that, I mean we ask a family member to view it with us and identify who's who and what's what. We select the best of the movies, and of the photographs, and then put it all together in our editing room. Later, oral recollections will be dubbed onto the video tape and a musical score of your choice is added. Are you following me so far?"

Brad nodded. "Just don't use words longer than three syllables and I should be all right," he replied mockingly.

"I simply meant that to someone unfamiliar with the production process it can be confusing."

"Wiring a hundred-foot schooner with heat sensors is confusing. This is child's play."

"It makes our child's play—" she used the words deliberately "—easier if you have a lot of material to work with. Does your family have that? Early photographs? Home movies?"

"What's the matter?" he countered. "Think we were too poor to own a camera?"

"I've spoken to very wealthy families that never bothered taking photos or having them taken." She'd been born into one of those families. "The term rich or poor is a relative one."

"Sure it is. If you've got money. Otherwise it means the difference between having a roof over your head and being out on the street."

"We're straying from the subject."

Brad picked up a pencil and began absentmindedly tapping it on his desk. "My grandparents won a movie camera in some contest when I was a kid, so there are plenty of home movies. Tons of them. And they also have several boxes of photographs dating back to the early twenties."

"That's great." She forced her gaze away from the lean lines of his fingers. "While making the family chronicles we usually don't shoot new footage of family members. The interviews are for the oral narration. What we're basically doing is compiling and reediting what you already have into a more viewable and enjoyable format. The video becomes a keepsake documentary of your family's unique story."

"Fine. I'll take one," he said.

"You will?"

"Why the surprised look?"

"I didn't think you'd be this easy to convince."

"There are times when I'm easy, and times when I'm hard."

The mental image his words conjured up were enough to make Sabrina shift in her chair. "We didn't discuss cost..." She gave him an amount.

Brad didn't blink an eye. "I can afford it."

She could tell from the edge to his voice that he resented her question. He certainly had a chip—no, make that a large continent—on his shoulder where money was concerned. "Then I'll fill out a work order." She uncapped her fountain pen. "When is your grandparents' anniversary?"

"The end of September."

Sabrina checked her calendar. It was now early August. "Okay." She nodded briskly. "That gives us almost two months. First I'd like you to give me the home movies you have and I'll arrange to have them transferred onto video tape. Meanwhile you and your other family members should go through and select your favorites from the early photographs and any slides you might have."

"I'll have the home movies ready for you tomorrow."

"You work fast."

You ain't seen nothin' yet, Brad thought to himself with anticipation.

"You can wait until the beginning of the week if you'd rather," Sabrina said, handing him the work order for his signature. "It might take longer for you to locate all the home movies. You don't want to miss anything."

"We Romanovskis are very thorough," Brad murmured. "I won't miss anything." He tapped the top line. "You spelled my name incorrectly."

"I did?"

"Yes. There's an *a* after the *m*, not an *o*."

"Sorry about that." Flushing, she took the paper back and made the correction.

This time when she handed him the paper his eyes were on her, rather than on the document. "Is that better?" she inquired defensively.

Nodding, he signed it and handed it back to her.

"Yes, well..." Sabrina began gathering her papers together.

"You seem in a hurry to leave," he noted. "Why? Could it be you're afraid to talk over old times?"

"What old times? We never had any old times."

"Exactly. I wonder why that was? Could it have had something to do with the fact that I was a grease monkey who fixed cars, while you were the Golden Girl of the country club set?"

"More likely it had something to do with the way you were constantly making fun of me," she retorted.

"Poor baby."

Sabrina felt an almost overwhelming urge to sock him one. Hard.

Sabrina's anger was apparent on her face. She had a very expressive face, Brad noted. He liked seeing the fire in her blue eyes and the flush on her classy cheekbones.

"You know, Brad, you haven't changed one bit," she said. Her tone of voice let him know that her comment was not a compliment.

"Oh, I've changed," he replied. He leaned forward. "Now I go after what I want."

She wasn't about to let him intimidate her. "So do I. And I avoid what I *don't* want."

Brad smiled. This was better than he'd anticipated. She was no longer retreating into her icy ivory tower. No. She'd actually come down to do battle with him. He liked that. "You also avoid what you're afraid of."

"If that's your way of insinuating that I'm afraid of you, you couldn't be more wrong. I'm not a vulnerable teenager, anymore."

"You were *never* a vulnerable teenager. You were a rich one."

"Is that why you were rude to me?" she demanded. "Because I was rich?"

"Because you were selfish and spoiled rotten."

"And you could tell all that from thirty feet away?" Sabrina retorted with mocking disbelief. "Amazing. And completely untrue. You didn't know the first thing about me! You never even spoke to me."

"You spoke *about* me, though. With your ritzy friends. Whenever they came to pick up their cars from the garage where I worked, they took great delight in telling me what you said."

Sabrina flushed. While she didn't remember exactly what she might have said about him so many years ago, she could imagine that none of it would have been very complimentary. He'd aggravated the daylights out of her in those days. He still did.

"As I said before," she said stiffly, "I don't see that there's any use in rehashing old history."

"What about more recent history? Like what you're doing back in Newport?"

"I'm working," she replied. "Same as you."

"Meaning we have something in common?"

"I imagine we have several things in common. We both breathe air, read from left to right and speak English. That doesn't necessarily mean that we'll ever get along."

"You give up too easily," Brad told her.

"Not at all. I'm not even entering this contest, so the term *giving up* doesn't apply here. We're going to be working together, that's all."

"Think you can handle that?" he taunted her.

"I'm a professional. I've worked with a lot of difficult people over the past few years. I'll manage."

"You've been working for a few years?"

"What did you think I've been doing for the past eight years? No, let me guess. You thought I was living la dolce vita, right? Indulging in all kinds of excesses and hedonistic pleasure. Gee, sorry to disappoint you."

"I don't think you're going to disappoint me, Golden Girl," Brad returned softly, meaningfully. "Not at all."

"I'm not a girl any longer. I'm twenty-nine. All grown-up, in case you hadn't noticed."

"Oh, I noticed, all right. And you've grown up, as you put it, very nicely, indeed."

He gave her one of *those* looks, the kind he'd been so good at giving her throughout her teenage years. Only this time there was a new element of speculation and male appreciation in his eyes. This time it was the look of a grown man, not a rebellious young stud on the prowl.

Sabrina's breath caught. She could practically feel the progression of his gaze, from her eyes to her lips. She watched his eyes lower to the small pearl buttons adorning the front of her dress. She could tell that he liked what he saw. Her breathing became hurried. There was no way to disguise the rapid rise and fall of her breasts.

"I'm late for my next appointment," she stated, latching on to that excuse with something close to desperation. "Give me a call when you have those home movies in hand."

"I'll be in touch." He drew the last word out, and the warmth of his appraisal gave it new meaning. Without taking his eyes from hers, Brad got up and walked around the desk.

Rattled, Sabrina stood also, not realizing that a pile of papers was still loose on her lap. They slid to the floor in a swirly avalanche of color.

"Here. Let me," Brad offered, hunkering down to gather the papers for her.

But Sabrina had already knelt down to pick them up herself. Their hands met over the form he'd signed moments ago. Sabrina froze. At the instant of contact, heat lightning flashed between them. It was elemental. Sensual. Intense.

Her eyes flew to his. Their fingers remained intertwined, generating even more heat. She felt the brush of his thumb over the top of her hand and marveled, then panicked, at the strength of her response. Who would have thought that such a simple touch could give rise to such complicated desires? Certainly not her. Nothing like this had ever happened to her before.

Brad saw the confusion reflected in her blue eyes and was encouraged by it. "This could get interesting," he murmured.

Sabrina tugged her hand away. "No, it can't," she stated firmly, quickly gathering the remaining papers and haphazardly stuffing them into her portfolio. "Not interesting at all. Or interested."

"No?"

"No," she repeated.

"Too bad I don't believe you."

Too bad indeed, Sabrina thought to herself, as she made her departure. She could definitely be in trouble here. Deep trouble.

"You survived!" Eliot greeted Sabrina upon her return to Memories. "Good. I was beginning to get worried."

He wasn't the only one, Sabrina thought to herself. She was pretty worried herself—about what had happened back there in Brad's office. What *had* happened? Her heart had raced. Her brain had refused to function. She'd felt as if she'd been hit by a cyclone and been left reeling in the wind. What was it about Brad that made her react that way?

Searching for an answer, she looked at Eliot. After Brad's forceful presence, Eliot seemed to pale in comparison. She decided that it was rather like putting a bicycle next to a Harley-Davidson motorcycle. One tended to overwhelm the other.

Sabrina knew that Brad was good at overwhelming. He'd done it to her from ten yards away as a teenager and he was still trying to do it to her now, eight years later.

What was it, she wondered, that made one man so different from the other? Eliot was older than Brad by at least ten years, yet he lacked the other man's aura of dynamic authority. With his neatly trimmed mustache and wire-rimmed glasses, Eliot was the epitome of class and sophistication. Even his fingernails were neatly manicured. His movements were controlled and orderly.

There was nothing controlled or orderly about Brad. He was as elemental as a thunderstorm and as unpredictable. He made an unforgettable impression. Yes, Brad was another kettle of fish entirely.

The phrase reminded her of that mounted fish on his wall. She wondered if he'd caught it himself. Probably with his bare hands, no less. The mental image made her smile. She pictured Brad landing the fish by simply ordering it, in that rough voice of his, to jump into his boat. What fish would dare disobey?

A smart fish. Like you. You're not going to jump to Brad's bidding. He's not going to land you, so you don't have to worry about ending up on a trophy wall next to that one-eyed fish. Her self-assurances were interrupted by the sound of Eliot's voice.

"So how did it go?" he asked her.

"Brad Romanovski actually signed up for one of our family chronicle packages," Sabrina replied.

"You sound surprised," Eliot noted.

"I am. I thought he was just insisting that I keep our appointment so that he could give me a hard time."

"And did he give you a hard time?"

"Yes." Reaching into her portfolio, she held up the contract. "But he also signed on the dotted line."

Only then did Sabrina notice what he'd added below his signature. In bold print he'd written the words "Providing Sabrina Stewart handles the job. No substitutions."

It was the first time she'd ever seen his handwriting. The slope of the letters reflected the energetic impatience of the man. But nothing could capture his aggravating stubbornness or exasperating roguery. "He put a proviso on here, do you believe it?" She handed the contract to Eliot.

He read what Brad had written and chuckled. "The man knows what he wants."

Eliot's words were eerily close to those Brad had spoken as he'd leaned toward her over his desk. *Now I go after what I want.* "He wants what he can't have," she retorted.

"This guy really gets to you, doesn't he? You've handled difficult clients before and never gotten flustered."

"Brad has raised being difficult to a fine art. However, I can handle it. Don't worry. I'm not about to let him get to me."

"Sounds like he already has."

"We had a few tense moments..." She paused, recalling with disconcerting clarity the brush of his hand over hers. Without even realizing it, she began rubbing her fingers, which had actually tingled when he'd touched them. "But I think we both made our positions clear. My only interest is in making this film for his grandparents' anniversary."

"Did he buy that?"

"He had no choice."

"Did you talk over old times?" Eliot asked.

"As a matter of fact, he did bring up the subject," Sabrina reluctantly admitted, "although I pointed out that we'd never really shared any time together."

"Think you cleared the air any?"

"I think he still harbors a lot of resentment against rich people. And that surprises me, given his current status and occupation. I mean, he must be dealing with wealthy people all the time in his line of work. It takes a lot of money to maintain a boat these days. We're not talking about a minor purchase here."

"I did a little checking up on him while you were gone," Eliot confessed.

"You wanted to make sure he wouldn't murder me in his office?" Sabrina inquired dryly.

"Something like that," Eliot agreed with a smile. "Anyway, Brad has a reputation for being direct and as honest as the day is long. He has 'a disdain for artifice'—Grace Fordham's words, not mine." Grace Fordham was one of the great dames of Newport society. She knew everyone there was to know. "He doesn't suffer fools gladly, is stubborn and proud. Has a temper which you arouse at your own risk. Holds a grudge when he feels he's been given just cause."

"I already guessed that he's capable of holding a grudge," Sabrina said. "He appears to be holding one against me. He made his opinion pretty clear. Accused me of being a spoiled rich kid."

"Maybe if you told him about the change in your family's circumstances, he might go easier on you," Eliot suggested.

"I have no intention of telling him that I no longer qualify as rich. It's none of his business."

"But it might help ease the tension between you if he realized you were no longer wealthy."

"The tension between us runs too deep to be that easily erased," Sabrina stated. "Brad isn't ruled by logic. He goes on instincts and emotions. Facts aren't always relevant."

"Yes, but maybe if you told him about your parents..."

"What should I tell him? That my parents are devoted environmentalists who have eschewed the evils of money by giving all theirs to an environmental group? That, for all intents and purposes, the Stewart family is now flat broke?" Sabrina shook her head. "No, thank you. I've seen the looks I get from the other people who know what my parents did. It's always accompanied by a questioning look, as if to say 'I wonder if insanity runs in the family.' I can do without that, thank you very much. Besides, Brad would just think I was playing some poor-little-rich-girl act. He already accused me of as much. Empathy isn't exactly his middle name, you know."

"If you think this job is going to be too difficult..."

"No, I'm not going to let him win," Sabrina said. "He's not going to scare me off again. This time I'm standing my ground. Brad can say whatever he likes. I'm going to stay cool, calm and collected."

Three

"She was so damn cool and collected in the beginning...it irritated the hell out of me...you know what I mean?" Brad looked to his old fishing buddy, Al Delvechio, for confirmation.

Al shrugged. "Hey, I just stopped by to see if we were still on to go fishing Sunday morning. I hear the blues are really biting. I don't know anything about this lady. You planning on setting bait for her or what?"

"I'd love to reel her in," Brad admitted.

"What's stopping you?"

"I knew her when I was a teenager. She wouldn't give me the time of day then."

"Ah. The one who got away. Now I get it. What's she look like?"

"Long blond hair, blue eyes, great body."

"Not married, is she?"

Brad shook his head. "I checked her ring finger first thing."

"Any guy waiting in the wings?"

"I don't think so. She hasn't been back in town that long. Still, I'll check it out. Not that it would make any difference."

"You think you've got a chance?" Al asked.

"It looks promising."

"Yeah?" Al moved his chair closer. "Tell me what happened."

"Chemistry, my friend. Plenty of chemistry."

"You lucky dog, you! It's every guy's fantasy to land the one that got away. Looks like here's your chance."

"I've waited a long time for this," Brad murmured.

"Just make sure she doesn't snag your line," Al cautioned him.

"She'll try. But I've got experience on my side."

"Yeah, the ladies always fall for you like a ton of bricks. The wife tells me you've got bedroom eyes, whatever the hell that means."

"It means that Sabrina Stewart had better watch her step. 'Cause I'm coming after her," Brad stated. "And I plan on getting her."

"I'm home," Sabrina announced as she closed the front door to her apartment and kicked off her shoes. Be it ever so humble, there was no place like *her* place. She was rather proud of the way she'd made it her own—from the wooden rocking chair she'd picked up at a garage sale to the linen drapes she'd sewn for the windows from a roll of remnant material. And scattered everywhere were mementos from her travels: a delicate Navajo bowl from out west; a wooden carving from Thailand; a blown-glass octopus from Venice. "Where are you, Thomas?"

A large marmalade-colored tomcat strolled into the living room, pausing to stretch and yawn before meandering on over.

"I can tell you've had another tough day," she teased, leaning down to rub the cat's ears. "Well, have you cooked my dinner and got it waiting for me on the table?"

"Meow."

"No such luck, huh? I guess it's salad again tonight. Not for you," she added as the cat meowed in protest. "I know you hate anything green, unless it's grass. Which reminds me, I brought you something." Sabrina pulled a handful of grass from her portfolio. "I don't think anyone saw me snitch this from out front. Hey, watch my fingers!"

The cat eagerly chomped on the green blades as if they were raw steak.

Sabrina prepared a shrimp salad for herself. There was no time to dawdle over dinner because there were dishes to be done and the wash to toss into the machine downstairs, not to mention the fact that the place hadn't been dusted in a week. Or was it two? Sabrina only knew that she could just about write her name on the furniture. And she had a stack of bills to get out, plus an inch of junk mail to go through.

All this after having put in a ten-hour work day. She'd already been tired when she'd come home. All she'd really wanted to do was go to bed. Instead she completed the household chores and then plopped on the couch for a moment's rest as she debated over whether or not the carpet could go another day without vacuuming.

She'd only been horizontal for thirty seconds when the phone rang. The modern convenience had been blissfully quiet for the past few hours, no doubt because she'd only discovered a few minutes ago that the bedroom extension had been off the hook.

"Hello?"

"Your line's been busy for the past three hours!"

Sabrina frowned at the cordless phone she was holding. "Who is this?"

"Who do you think it is, Golden Girl?"

She plopped back onto the couch. She had to conserve her energy. She couldn't afford to let her defenses down with Brad. Besides she was too tired to be angry with him and stand up at the same time. "How did you get my home phone number?"

"I looked it up in the phone book. Your number was busy for so long that I had the operator see if your line was out of order. He checked it and no one was talking. What did you do, take it off the hook?"

"Thomas knocked it off the hook. He likes doing that."

Brad felt himself clenching the telephone receiver a little tighter. "Who is Thomas?" And why the hell had he taken the phone off the hook? Brad wondered, as if he didn't already know. Damn! Could Sabrina be tied up with someone else already?

"Thomas is a very good friend of mine," she replied.

"How good?"

"Why are you calling me?"

Brad ignored her question. "Are you two living together?"

"Yes."

"I can't believe it! You're only back in town a few months and already you're living with some guy named Thomas?"

"I never said Thomas was a guy."

"You're living with a girl named Thomas?"

"I'm living with a cat named Thomas." Now why had she told him that? Sabrina irritably chastised herself. She should have kept quiet and let him think she was living with another man. It would have been the perfect protection. But it would also have been a lie and Sabrina hated to lie. Even to someone as aggravating as Brad.

Irked at being so damned honest, her voice was brisk as she got right to the point. "What do you want?"

"You." He paused for effect. "In my office. Tomorrow afternoon at three."

"What for?" she asked suspiciously.

"An afternoon of sexual pleasure?"

"Forget it!"

"Then how about for picking up the eight-millimeter family movies? I got them from my grandparents' house. They can't wait to meet you. I've been instructed to ask you when you plan on interviewing them."

The idea of Brad being instructed to do anything made her laugh.

"What's so funny?" he demanded defensively.

"I'm finding it a little hard picturing you being told what to do, let alone doing it."

"All the more reason for you to meet my grandparents. Come on, admit it. Aren't you just a tad bit curious about these people who not only order me around, but live to talk about it?"

"I'll admit, I am just a little bit curious."

"And I'm just dying to satisfy your curiosity," he huskily assured her.

"I was referring to your grandparents."

"So was I," he returned with an innocence she knew had to be contrived.

Sabrina reached for her schedule book, which was never far from her side. "How about next Wednesday?"

"How about tomorrow?"

"What's the big hurry?"

"My grandparents are impatient people."

"Is that where you get it from?" she inquired.

"Yep. I come by it honestly."

"So it would appear. I can't make it tomorrow but I do have some time on Saturday afternoon."

"That will have to do, I suppose. But I want to get rid of these movies before that."

Sabrina consulted her schedule. If she skipped lunch... "I can pick them up tomorrow around noon."

"Fine. Then we'll go out to lunch together."

"No, we won't."

"Don't tell me. Let me guess. You don't date clients, right?"

"Right."

"Sounds like the kind of excuse you'd come up with."

"It's not an excuse. It's the truth."

"It's a way for you to avoid facing what happened between us today."

"Nothing happened, aside from our airing our differing opinions of the past."

"You can ignore it, but it won't go away."

What he was really saying was that she could ignore *him* but *he* wouldn't go away. Sabrina knew that, yet she still said, "I don't know what you're talking about."

"And playing dumb won't wash, either," he added.

"Gee, Brad, if you talk this sweet to all the women you invite out it's no wonder that you're free for lunch."

She was just waiting for him to say that old line—*I'm not free but I can be had*. To her surprise, he picked up on the first part of her comment instead. "Oh, I can sweet-talk as well as the next guy, Golden Girl. Just wait and see."

Sabrina felt this sexual banter had gone on long enough. "Brad, our relationship is strictly business."

"I know that."

"Good. That means no more provocative comments."

"It means I'll do whatever it takes to make this business relationship personal," he corrected her.

Sabrina sighed. "I would have thought that you'd outgrown these kinds of adolescent games."

"There's nothing adolescent about my plans for you," he assured her in a husky murmur. "As I told you earlier today, some games get better as you get older. You told me you didn't know about that. I plan on teaching you."

"And I plan on avoiding you."

"Can't do that. We have business to conduct," he reminded her. "And a contract."

"Is this your way of punishing me?" Sabrina demanded.

"Punishing you for what?" he countered.

"I have no idea. Why don't you tell me."

"Hey, if you think lunch with me is my way of punishing you, then we'll forget about it," he declared.

"Fine."

"We can do dinner instead," he added teasingly.

Realizing she'd been set up, Sabrina told herself she was not amused. It wasn't true, though. "You're impossible!"

"My grandmother tells me I come by that honestly, too."

"Don't tell me the rest of your family is as..."

"Charming, attractive, sexy..." he helpfully supplied.

"Stubborn, dogmatic and determined as you are."

"'Fraid so."

"How encouraging."

"Hey, if it's encouragement you want—"

"I don't want anything," Sabrina stated.

"Well, my grandparents want something. They want to meet you. We never did set a time on Saturday."

"One in the afternoon."

"Sounds good. I'll see you there at one."

"Wait a second! There's no need for you to be present. I'm sure your grandparents and I can manage without you."

"I'm sure you can, but there's no chance in hell I'm going to let you. You might as well get used to the idea. I plan on being right there, making sure they don't drag out that photo of me bare-bottomed on the living room floor."

"Another one of your teenage pranks?" she inquired sweetly.

She heard his chuckle over the phone line and was amazed at how sexy it sounded. Like the rough purr of a mountain cat. "Nice try, Golden Girl. I was six months old at the time."

"I wish you wouldn't call me that."

"Why not?"

"It bothers me."

"You prefer Golden Lady?"

"I prefer my name. Sabrina."

"It's a nice name. Classy and sexy. Like you."

Trust him to turn something as innocuous as her name into a lesson in seduction. He really was a rogue. Which got her to thinking... "What did your grandparents think of your carousing teenage years?" She spoke her thoughts aloud.

"Where did that question come from?" he said.

"Are you going to answer it or not?"

"Not."

"So they didn't approve." That idea pleased her. She didn't like to think she was the only one who disapproved of his ways.

"I never said that."

"You didn't have to. The way you avoided answering the question answered it for you."

"Which is exactly what I've been saying about you. The way you avoid talking about what happened between us in my office this afternoon answers the question for you, too."

She'd fallen right into that trap. "Brad, I'm not an impressionable teenager any longer. You can't intimidate me anymore."

"Why should I want to intimidate you? Believe me there are plenty of other things I'd rather do to you. Want me to tell you about them?"

"No!"

He chuckled softly. "I didn't think so. The truth is that I'm enjoying our little battles. And so are you, only you're not ready to admit it yet. Think about it. I'll see you tomorrow."

He hung up without saying goodbye, but even more aggravating, he was right about her enjoying their verbal battles. They made her feel breathless and alive. *He* made her feel that way. Which wasn't a good sign.

* * *

"I'm here to pick up some reels of film," Sabrina briskly informed Brad's secretary.

"Brad's been waiting for you. He said I should have you go on into his office."

Darn. She'd been hoping he'd have the good sense to leave the film with his secretary for her to pick up. No such luck.

He was on the phone when she entered his office. He had what appeared to be a series of blueprints of boat specifications rolled out on the desk in front of him.

"I think a simple code system hooked to the ignition would be best in your case," Brad was saying. "The hidden cameras I installed in your brother-in-law's yacht wouldn't be cost efficient for you." He waved Sabrina into the chair she'd occupied yesterday and indicated that he'd be with her in a minute. "Sure, we can have sirens and lights going off if the system is tampered with. Horns, too, if you'd like."

Today Brad's shirt was a dark teal blue. The buttons at the shirt collar were opened and there was no sign of a tie. He looked good in dark colors. Obviously he still favored them. The same way he favored sultry brunettes? she wondered.

Heeding the danger signs flashing in her mind, she resolutely looked away from Brad and studied his office instead of him. She was less likely to run into trouble that way.

When she'd entered the room yesterday, the stuffed fish on the wall had been the only thing she'd really noticed. Other than Brad, that is. Now she ignored both him and the fish, and focused on the rest of the room.

Despite the fact that Brad appeared to have forsaken wearing a business suit, his office was very businesslike—complete with fax machine and personal computer. She also discovered two small round windows that resembled portholes, from which there was a nice view of the harbor.

A second later Brad was blocking that view as he stood in front of her. "Sure you won't reconsider lunch? You don't know what you're missing."

"Yes, I do."

Her retort did nothing to dampen the amusement in his eyes. If anything, that amusement only grew. "And yet you turned me down, anyway? How self-sacrificing of you." To her relief he didn't dwell on the matter, but turned over the box of film without any further ado. "I also included a map in there so you can find my grandparents' place," he told her. "It's in Middletown. I'm assuming you're going to insist on driving there yourself rather than letting me drive you?"

"You assume correctly."

"See? Only together again for two days and already I'm getting to know your little idiosyncrasies."

"How astute of you."

"Yeah, that's me. A real astute kind of guy."

"Modest, too."

"Hey, buddy, you ready for lunch?" a burly man demanded from the doorway.

"Yeah, Al, I'll be right with you."

"Aren't you going to introduce me?" the man inquired.

"Al Delvechio, Sabrina Stewart."

Sabrina wondered if she'd imagined the thumbs-up sign the man flashed Brad. "Nice to meet you," she murmured. "I've got to get going." But on her way out she sneaked one last look over her shoulder. Sure enough, Al was slapping Brad's hand the way football players did to congratulate one another when they caught an interception. She was not reassured.

Sabrina had no problem finding Brad's grandparents' house. Brad's map was clear and direct. He'd drawn it with the skill of a navigator, even including a little north-south, east-west symbol in the corner. He was waiting for her when she pulled up in front of the small Cape-Cod-style house.

He was dressed in his trademark dark colors—navy-blue shirt and new-looking blue jeans. Even the baseball cap he wore was blue and displayed the insignia of the New York Mets.

To her surprise Brad walked over and opened her car door for her. "I see you made it all right," he noted.

She wanted to ignore the hand he held out to assist her, but knew that was what he was expecting of her. So she accepted it instead. She expected her fingers to tingle the second he touched them, and sure enough, they did.

Brad's grandparents, however, weren't at all what she expected. They were standing by the front door, ready to greet them. Brad's grandfather looked like the spitting image of Santa Claus, complete with white beard and twinkling blue eyes. He was wearing a Chicago Cubs T-shirt. She'd expected someone more imposing, less cuddly.

As for his grandmother, she was a lively looking lady with arresting light blue eyes. Her short, dark hair showed only the slightest hint of silver.

"You still rooting for those good-for-nothing Mets?" the older man demanded of Brad before they'd even entered the house. "He wears that cap just to aggravate me, you know," he added for Sabrina's benefit.

"Sabrina Stewart, meet my grandfather Joseph Romanovski, a misguided Cubs fan."

"How a grandson of mine could like the Mets is beyond me," Joseph grumbled. "It must be from your mother's side of the family. They were from New York City. Brainwashed you as a child. You a Mets fan, too?" Joseph questioned Sabrina.

"No. I don't follow baseball much," Sabrina admitted.

"Well, that's something, I suppose," he said.

"Stop with all the sports talk, would you please? Come in, come in. I'm Violet, Bradley's grandmother. Sit down, my dear. Would you like some iced tea?"

"That would be nice," Sabrina replied. So Brad's full name was Bradley, hmm? Interesting. "Thank you."

"I made the iced tea," Joseph inserted. "Special recipe. I let it sit in the sun."

"It's very good," Sabrina noted after taking a sip.

"So, my dear..." Violet sat on the couch next to her husband and gave Sabrina a look of kindly benevolence. "Bradley tells us that you used to spend your summers in Newport."

"That's right. We lived in Boston the rest of the year, but we had a summer house here."

"The Vanderbilts had a summer house here," Joseph inserted. "Has something like one hundred rooms in it."

"I know." Sabrina's voice reflected her enthusiasm. Newport's colorful history had long been a favorite topic of hers. "I've visited The Breakers. It's amazing. If that was just their summer cottage, it makes you wonder what their city house in New York must have looked like. It's a shame that one was knocked down."

"Memorials to the rich *should* be knocked down," Brad stated.

"Newport's mansions are an irreplaceable piece of American history," Sabrina protested indignantly.

"Built by the sweat of the working class."

"The pyramids were built by the sweat of slaves. Does that mean you think they should be knocked down?" she countered.

"I saw a special on TV about the pyramids," Joseph inserted. "Very impressive, it was. Very impressive indeed. Always wanted to go there. And now that I think about it, The Breakers has seventy rooms. Just wanted to straighten that out."

Joseph's comment momentarily stopped the flow of conversation.

After an awkward pause, Violet turned to ask Sabrina, "Have you done a lot of traveling?"

"A fair amount."

"Tell me about some of your favorite places."

"Bermuda is lovely but I guess I'd have to say that the Alps are my favorite place."

"Did you travel alone or with your family?"

"Both," Sabrina replied. "My parents tend to enjoy more remote locations, however. Like the rain forest."

"They're cutting the forests down, you know. I saw it on TV," Joseph said.

"I know they are." Sabrina's parents had put a lot of money into rain forest conservation efforts. "It's something we should all be concerned about. Those forests are being cut down at the rate of fifty to one hundred acres a minute! If that continues the world's rain forests will disappear completely from many nations by the year 2000, less than a decade away."

"That's what they said on the TV," Joseph agreed.

"And when the rain forests disappear," Sabrina continued, "so will all the animals that depend upon those forests for their sustenance and shelter. Some scientists say that up to one-fifth of all species of life on this planet would disappear. That would be the most massive extinction of wildlife since the disappearance of the dinosaurs! And that's not all. Think of all the plants that would disappear, many of which already provide or could in the future provide cures to some of our worst diseases."

"I had no idea," Violet murmured. "I never thought of that."

"Then there's the matter of the role the rain forests play in stabilizing global climate patterns," Sabrina said. "Scientists are just beginning to study how the widespread destruction of the world's rain forests might affect the levels of carbon dioxide in the air, raising it enough to increase the Earth's temperature. That kind of global warming would have enormous consequences."

"Global warming, hmmm?" Joseph stroked his chin thoughtfully. "It's been a hot summer, that's for sure. Sounds like you know what you're talking about, young lady."

"My parents are environmentalists," Sabrina admitted.

"It's a popular cause these days," Brad said, as if that were their only reason for being concerned.

"My parents aren't involved because it's popular," Sabrina replied. "They're involved because they care very passionately about the future of this planet. It's a full-time commitment for them." Very full-time. Almost to the exclusion of all else, including their daughter.

"Must be nice, not having to work for a living," Brad noted.

"They work harder than you or I do."

"Celebrity tennis tournaments, that sort of thing?" he inquired mockingly.

"Obviously you already know what you think," Sabrina said stiffly. "You don't want to be confused with facts."

"Bradley, it's impolite to pick on Sabrina's parents that way," Violet reprimanded him. "I'm sure they're very nice people. How about brothers and sisters, Sabrina? Do you have any?"

"No. I'm an only child."

Sabrina could practically read Brad's thoughts. Spoiled, only child. Rich, spoiled, only child. If he only knew... But he never would, because she didn't plan on telling him a thing about her private life.

She turned her attention back to his grandparents. "Speaking of children, I brought along this family chart for you to fill out. If you could list the names of your children and their spouses, as well as your grandchildren and their spouses it would make things easier."

Joseph took the form while Violet noted, "It must be exciting doing what you do."

"I enjoy it," Sabrina confirmed.

"In my day, women didn't have careers," Violet said regretfully. "Although I must confess that when I was younger I dreamed of being an artist. That or a truck driver."

"I never knew that," Brad said, looking at his grandmother in surprise.

"Oh, yes." Violet smiled. "I wanted to travel, and driving across the country in a truck seemed very romantic to me at the time. I thought it would be great to be able to stop and paint the beautiful scenery along the way."

"Then she met me," Joseph said. "We were married within three months."

"He sort of swept me off my feet," Violet admitted.

"No *sort of* about it," Joseph said. "That was almost fifty years ago. I wouldn't take no for an answer. I'll tell you this much, that's one thing this family's got. Perseverance. *Can't* is a four-letter word in our book. I taught Brad's father that and he taught Brad that. Someday soon Brad will be teaching his kids that."

Sabrina was delighted to see Brad squirming in his seat. It was only a slight movement, but she caught it. She also caught the loving look Violet was giving him.

"Brad's a Scorpio," Violet said. "Tell him something can't be done and he'll do it, just to prove you wrong."

Interesting. I'll have to file that for future reference, Sabrina told herself. Was that why he'd been pursuing her? Because she'd said no? She would have questioned Violet further about this character trait of Brad's but Joseph began speaking first.

"That horoscope stuff's got nothing to do with it. I'm telling you, it's because he's a Romanovski," Joseph stated. "It's in his blood. Same way working with boats is in his blood. I spent most of my life working in the boat yards, so has my son. Brad here's the first one to break out on his own though. You like to sail?" Joseph asked Sabrina.

"I haven't done much sailing."

Three pairs of eyes turned to her with varying degrees of surprise. "Not done much sailing?"

She shrugged. "Boats and I don't get along very well. They tend to make me seasick." She also couldn't swim, a gap in her education she wasn't in the habit of disclosing.

"They've got ways of treating seasickness," Brad said. "You shouldn't let that keep you from enjoying the ocean."

"I enjoy the ocean. I have a lovely view from my apartment building." The view wasn't from *her* apartment, however. That would have added much more to the rent. "And I enjoy taking a walk along the Cliff Walk. You can get some great views from there."

"Yes, but it's not the same as being out there on the water," Brad maintained.

"I know," Sabrina agreed. "That's why I like it."

Brad didn't know why, but he had a funny feeling that a queasy stomach wasn't the only thing keeping her a landlubber. "Not afraid of the water are you?"

"Of course not!"

"You do much swimming?"

"No."

"Why not?"

"I never learned how." Her father had once promised to teach her, but had never followed through. Once she got older she'd meant to take lessons but hadn't gotten around to it. "I don't know how to swim, okay?" she admitted in exasperation. "It's no big deal."

Bingo. Brad had known there had to be something else. He was pleased to discover that his instincts were right on target where she was concerned.

"Everyone should know how to swim," Brad stated. "I'll teach you how."

In your dreams! The thought went unspoken as Sabrina smiled politely and declined his offer. "But enough about me. What about you two?" she asked Brad's grandparents. "Did you have any questions about the video?"

"You do a lot of these?" Joseph asked.

"A fair number," she replied. "They're becoming very popular."

"You could have knocked us down with a feather when Bradley told us what he was planning," Violet said.

"I think it's a great idea," Joseph added. "We Romanovskis have a very colorful past. Why, my grandmother was a courtesan in the Russian Court."

"Your background is Russian?" Sabrina asked.

"No. Polish," Joseph replied. "Good ship builders. Mostly good peasant stock. Except my grandmother. The stories I heard about her..." He then went on to relate a few of them.

The time passed quickly and before she knew it, it was time for Sabrina to leave. She had to videotape a Saturday-evening wedding in a few hours.

"Your grandfather's quite a storyteller," Sabrina noted as Brad accompanied her to her car.

"What he doesn't remember, he makes up. Or so my grandmother says."

"His narrative will make that portion of the video all the more dramatic. By the way, the home movies should be transferred onto video tape by the middle of the week. I'll set up a date for going over them with you at that time."

"A date?"

"Purely a figurative word."

"Not in my book."

"The same book where *can't* is a four-letter word?" she inquired.

"That's the one. The Romanovski Family Manual. What about the Stewart Family Manual? What ritzy rules are in that book?"

"I don't think we have a family manual," she said regretfully. To have a family manual you had to have a strong sense of family: that certain bonding that comes from a loving relationship and powerful emotional ties. Her parents weren't interested in emotions, just in ecology.

Noticing the curious look Brad was giving her, Sabrina felt compelled to come up with something. She didn't want him asking about her family. "But if there were a manual, I bet recycling would be rule one." If anything, Brad's look became even more questioning, so she explained further. "Recycling to cut down on world pollution. You know, collecting your newspapers, glass bottles and sending them to recycling centers to be used again—that sort of thing. I guess that would be the Stewart family motto. Did you know that a glass bottle tossed onto the side of the road and left untouched could remain there for a million years without decomposing?"

"You trying to convert me?" he inquired with amusement.

"Do you need converting?"

"You really want to know what I need?" he murmured softly.

She hastily backed up a step.

"I didn't think so."

Irritated with herself for showing a moment's weakness, this time Sabrina stood her ground. "I think you need a keeper. Someone who'll keep you in line."

"You applying for the job?"

"Absolutely not."

He nodded understandingly. "Too much of a challenge for you, huh?"

"Too much of a hassle."

"Meaning you think I'd give you a hard time?"

"You've always given me a hard time. That's nothing new."

"Maybe not. But this..." He reached out to gently run his fingertip down her arm, which was left bare by the sleeveless blouse she wore. "This is something new."

She knew he was deliberately playing on the chemistry between them, but she refused to take the bait. She didn't pull away, but she didn't give in, either. Instead she responded with practical humor. It had always worked well for her in the past. "Actually, Brad, it's not new...I've had that arm for a long time now. Since I was born, in fact."

He smiled. "It's a very nice arm. Smooth. Soft."

"And strong," she added. "It has to be to tote video equipment around."

He looked at her in surprise. "They make you carry your own equipment?"

"No one *makes* me do anything. It's time you realized that, Brad. Remember it."

After she'd gotten in her car and driven away, Brad still stood there at the curb, smiling as he softly murmured, "Oh, I'll remember it all right, Golden Girl. Remember it and prove you wrong."

Four

Sabrina welcomed the break from Brad's company over the next few days. That didn't mean that she didn't think about him, however. It was hard not to when she got a preliminary look at some of the home movies once they'd been transferred. There Brad was, as a rambunctious three-year-old pushing a toy car. She recognized the devilish smile. Some things never changed, and Brad's smile was one of them.

Her reaction to him was another thing that hadn't changed. He still had some kind of strange power over her. Although she was pleased at the way she'd held her own when he'd touched her arm, the truth was that she'd felt the provocative brush of his fingertips for hours afterward. Even now, the memory of that moment made her feel warm and all stirred up inside.

It didn't help matters any that he was on his way over now to view the video tapes with her. That meant more time spent in close confines with him.

She checked her appearance in the mirror of her compact and nodded approvingly. At least her inner nervousness didn't show. She looked just the way she wanted to—calm and in control.

She'd chosen her outfit with that idea in mind. The navy blue rayon skirt was long enough to hide most of her legs from view. The jacket she wore was one of her favorites, navy blue with a classy foulard design of little hexagons in maroon and pink. She knew the shapes were hexagonal because she'd studied them closely earlier in the day when she'd been brooding about Brad and all the problems he presented. She'd had the jacket a year and had never been reduced to counting the sides of the geometric patterns before. This was what Brad had driven her to!

She made one final check to make sure that the square of pale pink silk peering up from her jacket pocket was unruffled. Just as she planned on being unruffled. She smoothed a wrinkle from the matching pink blouse she wore, then snapped her compact closed with a force that almost broke the mirror.

"That's all I'd need right now," she muttered to herself. "Seven years of bad luck."

When Brad arrived at Memories she was ready for him.

"I've got everything set up in the viewing room," she said. "I've made some notes of what I think might make some good footage. But I don't want to miss something important. So I'll show you the tapes and you can tell me relevant names, places and dates."

"Hello to you, too," Brad replied mockingly.

Not a real auspicious beginning, she had to admit. But the tension between them subsided once they sat down to view the tapes.

Brad found it strange seeing pictures of himself as a child on the large TV screen. The shot of him sticking his hand smack in the middle of what was obviously his first birthday cake drew a laugh from Sabrina.

She pushed the Pause button. "I thought this one would make a good addition. Note that your parents are in the background, probably telling you that you can't have your cake until after everyone sings 'Happy Birthday.'" There was no audio track on the eight-millimeter home movies, but Sabrina had no trouble reading the lips of his horrified parents. "Apparently the Romanovski rule worked in this case. Someone told you you couldn't do something and you proved them wrong."

Brad preferred remembering the yuppy banker who'd told him he couldn't make a go of a business specializing in marine security and him subsequently proving that the stuffed shirt was wrong. But he made no protest over the inclusion of his cake-smearing incident in the final compilation. He'd enjoyed the sound of Sabrina's laughter too much to regret whatever had caused it. Her laughter was husky... and as sexy as the rest of her.

He noticed that the skirt she wore today was much longer than the one she'd worn when she'd come to his office a week ago. He was willing to bet that the lower hemline was meant to be a deterrent. She probably didn't want him eyeing her legs.

Not that it made any difference. He eyed her anyway, admiring the way she walked as she crossed the room to answer a phone call. She still possessed that provocative sway of her hips, and the movement still had the power to make his mouth go dry. Even the way she sat was classy—the finishing-school propriety of her posture, shoulders thrown back, spine as straight as a ruler.

His own spine was starting to ache after a long day spent crouched in the cramped confines of a motor cruiser. The security system he was installing had not been cooperative. Neither was Sabrina.

He'd noticed the careful distance she kept between them. She'd deliberately avoided even the slightest brush of their hands. He knew why. He was getting to her.

Brad couldn't help feeling rather pleased with himself about that. Things were moving right along as planned. He'd baited the hook and she was just about ready to bite. Soon he'd be able to reel her in, slowly but surely. Then she'd be his.

And after that? His plans were still rather vague beyond that point. He could toss her back, or he could keep her. Either way, he would have proven his point and satisfied his inner need to avenge a wrong done to him.

The problem was that Brad was beginning to have other needs where Sabrina was concerned. And other thoughts of satisfaction!

Sabrina soon noticed his inattentiveness. "Have you seen enough for today? Or do you want to see more?"

He wanted to see more, a lot more... of her. He wanted to see her sprawled between satin sheets, his sheets. It didn't matter that he didn't own satin sheets. She made him want to go out and buy some. Right away. So that he could lay her down on them and make wickedly slow love to her.

"Brad?"

"Hmm?"

"I asked if you wanted to stop looking at the video tapes and finish this another day?"

"No. Let's keep going."

And they did. Determined to keep his mind on business rather than pleasure, Brad watched himself growing older on film—building his first snowman, welcoming his baby sister home, throwing his first football. He saw the family get-togethers, the summertime barbecues and the compulsory gather-round-the-Christmas-tree shots.

He supplied Sabrina with the information she needed: the dates, which cousin was which. She took pages of notes, marking the number displayed on the tape counter indicator for each scene to be included.

As Sabrina watched the tapes with him she was struck by the overwhelming sense of family stability with which he'd grown up. His upbringing might have lacked material wealth, but it had clearly been rich with emotional support. How different from her own background.

She'd have a hard time compiling a tape of her own family because, aside from the few professionally taken photographs to mark one or two milestone occasions, there weren't many photographs from her childhood. Her parents had preferred landscape photography. There were no people in their pictures. They had shots of their first sighting of a gray whale off the coast of Baja California, but no record of Sabrina's first snowman or her first day of school.

Looking at her in the soft light of the viewing room, Brad wondered what had caused her pensive look.

"What do you say we take a break?" he suggested. "I'm hungry. How about you?"

Sabrina nodded her agreement. She'd skipped lunch again today.

"I know a great little place down by the harbor that serves up some mean fried clams," he said. "You interested?"

"Yes."

She could tell by his slightly startled expression that he hadn't expected her to accept his invitation so readily. But she'd decided that if saying no only spurred him on, then maybe saying yes would be a more effective deterrent. She had to admit that it felt good to be throwing *him* for a change. Usually she was the one caught off guard.

"You appear surprised," she couldn't resist noting.

"I am. I wish I'd known sooner that the way to get you to accept a dinner date was to dangle the promise of fried clams in front of you."

"It's dinner, but it's not a date. I just want to clarify that."

"Right."

She could tell he didn't believe her for one minute. "We're going Dutch, and I'll drive my own car. Just give me the directions and I'll meet you there."

"I would have thought that with your environmentalist background, you'd want to conserve energy by going in one car."

"It might conserve gasoline, but it wouldn't necessarily conserve energy. *My* energy."

"You don't trust yourself alone in a car with me." Brad nodded understandingly. "I suppose I can understand that."

"You're right, I don't trust myself to be alone in a car with you. I might be tempted to do you great bodily harm for all the aggravation you've caused me over the years."

"Feel free to try," he invited her, spreading out his arms as if offering her free rein over his body. "Anytime."

"Thanks for the offer," she retorted dryly, "but all I'm interested in at the moment is food."

Holding the door open for her, Brad noted, "I guess my mom was right when she told me that the way to a woman's heart was through her stomach."

As Sabrina drove to the restaurant she reflected on Brad's teasing comment about a woman's heart. She knew he wasn't interested in her heart. She presented a challenge to him, that was all.

She looked into her rearview mirror, noticing the car behind her. Brad was following her to the restaurant. She'd expected him to be driving some updated version of the hot set of wheels he'd tooled around in as a teenager. Instead he drove a Bronco. She'd noticed it on the street near his grandparents' house, but had never attributed its ownership to him.

In that Bronco, Brad was still shaking his head over Sabrina's choice of car. He hadn't believed it when she'd pulled in front of his grandparents' house in an American-made, plain white sedan. It wasn't even a new model; in fact, it was several years old. At the time he'd decided it must have been a loaner, lent to her while her ritzy car was in the shop.

But here she was, still driving the sedate-looking economy model. Why? He'd pictured her driving some elegant foreign model that had the same kind of slinky curves she did. A Jaguar? Yeah, he thought she'd look great in a Jaguar. Or the black Corvette that he had at home. He'd come straight from the office. The Bronco was practical for work. The Corvette was strictly for fun.

Sabrina had already gotten out of her car by the time he joined her at the restaurant's parking lot. Noticing her hesitant look at the restaurant, he forgot to ask her about her car and instead defended his choice. "It may not be the fanciest place in the world, but it's got good food."

"I'm sure it does."

"Not quite the ritzy establishment you're used to, huh? No fine china, no crystal goblets, no maître d'. None of that fancy stuff that adds another twenty bucks to the price of the dinner. God forbid that this place should ever get trendy with the so-called In Set," he said as he held the restaurant's door open for her.

She shook her head at his taunt. "There you go again, biting the hand that feeds you." When he eyed her fingers suggestively, she hurriedly added, "I was speaking figuratively."

"Yeah. I noticed you tend to do that a lot," he said, taking her by the elbow and leading her to a nearby table. "What are you talking about this time?"

"I was referring to the fact that in the course of your work as a specialist in shipboard security systems—"

"What a mouthful," he inserted wryly.

"You must deal with a number of wealthy people. Owning a boat, let alone a yacht, is not an inexpensive proposition. Doesn't your somewhat hostile attitude toward the rich hamper your dealings with your clients?"

"I haven't received any complaints so far."

"Who would dare? You'd probably bite their heads off and toss them out of your office."

"Probably," he agreed with a grin.

"Hi, folks," a white-aproned waitress greeted them. "What'll you two have tonight?"

"Fried clams," Brad and Sabrina said in unison.

"That was easy," the waitress noted with a grin. "Anything to drink?"

"I'll have iced tea," Sabrina said. "And could we have two checks, please?"

"Sure. And you?" the waitress asked Brad.

"I'll have her check and a beer."

As soon as they were alone, Sabrina demanded, "What was that all about? We agreed to go Dutch."

"I never agreed to anything. What's the big deal, anyway? Consider it a working dinner."

"In that case the company should pay for the client's meal."

"Memories can pick up the tab next time. Just sit back and relax. You look like you're going to break if you bend just an inch. Don't you ever kick off your shoes and let go, every once in a while?"

"Of course I do. Just not in a public restaurant."

"Where *do* you let go?"

Sabrina spoke without thinking. "That's for me to know and you to find out."

"I aim to, believe me," he softly assured her.

"It was just an idle comment. Not a challenge. I was only kidding. I didn't intend to be taken literally."

"How about being taken slowly and seductively," Brad murmured. "How does that appeal?"

"I'd rather eat my dinner," she retorted as the waitress deposited their dishes in front of them.

"Shot down again—and by a dish of fried clams, no less!" Brad heaved an exaggerated sigh. "Of course, they *are* damn good clams. Caught fresh this morning, I'll bet." He contentedly munched on a mouthful.

Sabrina watched the movement of his angular jaw, the telltale movement of his Adam's apple as he swallowed.

How did he manage to make a simple thing like eating so incredibly sexy?

"Mmm, good," he proclaimed. "Definitely fresh." Noticing that she had yet to take a bite, he said, "What's the matter?"

"Nothing."

"Eat up. These are great."

He took another bite, another swallow, and closed his eyes in delight. Sabrina couldn't even blink. Her eyes remained fixed on him—only moving from his lips, to his jaw, to his throat and back again. This had to stop, she told herself. But he did have wonderful lips. Why hadn't she ever noticed them before?

When he opened his eyes and caught her staring at him, she had to say something. "Do you always put this much feeling into everything you do?"

"What's life without a little passion in it?"

She wondered if that's why he liked voluptuous, sultry brunettes. Because they had passion. Was it something she had? She wondered about that while eating her own clams. And she wondered about Brad, wondered what he'd been up to for the past eight years.

"You know, I was surprised when I found out you were still here in Newport," she admitted. "I pictured you working on the oil pipeline up in Alaska, or roughing it in some remote fishing village someplace."

"I can't say I wasn't tempted." He was delighted to hear that she'd pictured him doing something. That meant she'd thought about him.

"What made you choose this line of work?" Sabrina asked. "As I said before, given your less than appreciative views of people with money, I'd have thought that you'd go out of your way to avoid having to deal with them at all."

"I like my work. That's why I do it. But I don't like frivolous people who have more money than they know what to do with. Dealing with that type is just a pain in the rear end," Brad said bluntly. "True boating enthusiasts are one thing—I get along with them fine—but bored blue bloods with money to burn still drive me nuts."

Brad had come to blows with the type often enough when he'd been in high school. Then he'd been the lowly grease monkey who repaired their expensive cars or cleaned their rich parents' yachts down at the boat yard.

While Brad wasn't as hot-tempered now as he was then, that kind of condescending attitude still irritated the hell out of him. Fortunately very few of his clients treated him with anything other than respect. And if they did they didn't remain his clients for long.

"Luckily I don't have to deal with that type very often," he added, pushing away his empty plate. "Most of the people I work with all share a love for the ocean."

"Have you ever been tempted to take off on a yacht yourself?" she asked.

"I did. I crewed on a racing yacht for a while, then worked on a charter schooner in the Caribbean. Ended up working my way around the world for a year or two. Then came home to join my dad at the boat yards. Eventually I moved on to work with a yacht designer. Then I opened my own business."

"Eliot tells me you're doing very well at it."

"Who's Eliot?" Brad demanded.

"My boss. The owner of Memories."

"You two close?"

"Do you really think I'm going to answer that question?"

"You just did."

"Oh, I forgot," she noted mockingly. "You read minds—from ten yards away, no less. That's how you were able to tell that I was a spoiled, rich teenager, and no doubt that's how you know whether or not Eliot and I are close."

"I could tell you were spoiled by the way you acted and the people you hung out with."

"What did *I* ever do to indicate I was spoiled? Give me one example," she challenged him. "Something specific that I did, as opposed to the crowd I hung out with."

Brad was hard-pressed to come up with anything.

"There! I knew it!" she said triumphantly. "It wasn't anything I did."

"You showed lousy judgment in your choice of friends, among other things," he retorted.

Sabrina hated to admit that Brad was right. She'd run into a few of those friends since her return and had been amazed to find she didn't have anything in common with them anymore. They no longer shared the same interests or even the same values. Besides, her lowered financial status had resulted in an invisible but very real gap between herself and those so-called friends. Most of them weren't bad people, just a tad shallow. Especially Guy "Playboy-of-the-Western-World" Smythe-Jones.

"So you don't want to answer that observation, huh?" Brad noted with satisfaction.

Sabrina grinned as a sudden thought occurred to her. Leaning across the table, she murmured, "You know what I *really* want?"

Brad licked lips that had suddenly gone dry. She was looking at him with *such* anticipation...and she had a downright seductive gleam in those blue eyes of hers. "What do you want?"

"A turtle sundae! Vanilla ice cream smothered in chocolate syrup and caramel sauce with a generous sprinkling of pecans on top. Mmm, mmm, good..." She ran her tongue over her lips in a delicate, catlike motion. "I know a place down here by the harbor that has the best ice cream in the city. We could walk there, it's a nice night."

Brad knew when he'd been had. "You get this excited over an ice-cream sundae?"

Her grin widened. "As you said, what's life without a little passion in it? Besides, it's my favorite flavor. I've been craving one all day."

"Well, I certainly want to make sure all your cravings are satisfied. Any others you want to tell me about?"

"I like black olives and cheese curls, although not together."

"What, no caviar?"

She winkled her nose. "Absolutely, positively, no caviar!"

After she'd devoured her turtle sundae, Sabrina walked off the scrumptious dessert by strolling with Brad along the wharf. The boats were all lit up, as was the Newport Bridge.

"It's a beautiful view, isn't it?" she noted. "When the bridge is illuminated at night, it doesn't look real. All those glittering lights make it seem like some kind of fairy-tale creation stretched out across the water."

Sabrina was so involved with admiring the view that she didn't pay attention to where she was walking—a mistake on a wooden wharf. Before she knew what had happened, the high heel of her right shoe got wedged in between the slats of wood and she lunged forward. Had Brad not reacted quickly and caught her she might well have fallen flat on her face.

"If you wanted to be in my arms, all you had to do was ask," he murmured wickedly.

Sabrina hurriedly freed herself. "My shoe got caught." She slipped her foot out of the guilty shoe and reached down to try to free the heel.

"If you're not careful you're going to get a splinter in your bare foot," he warned her.

"It's not bare. I'm wearing nylons."

"Great protection against a splinter, I'm sure."

He was probably right. She lifted up her stockinged foot. Balancing on her other leg, she felt as awkward as a stork.

"Here." Brad knelt down and retrieved her shoe. He then curved his hand around the back of her calf and drew her foot to his bent knee. Oh, so slowly, he trailed his fingers down the curve of her leg until he reached her ankle, where his thumb moved in a provocative circle over the delicate bone. His touch was softly caressing. Her skin was tingling by the time he ultimately guided her foot into the shoe he held in his other hand.

"Thank you," she said in a slightly strangled voice. He'd caught her off guard. "I feel like Cinderella," she added with a nervous laugh. She also felt like she'd been hit with lightning!

He stood up. "Does that mean I'm Prince Charming?"

"You can be charming when you want to be," she acknowledged.

"Praise indeed coming from a ritzy lady like you."

"Are we actually complimenting each other?"

"I guess we are."

Their eyes met and their smile was shared. For Sabrina it was a powerful moment, for if she'd thought that the magic between her and Brad was strong before, she found it was downright irresistible now.

The gentle lapping of the water and the bump of the boats against the docks faded into the distance. All her senses were focused on Brad. He was standing so close to her that she could hear him breathing, feel the warmth of his body. He wasn't touching her with anything but his eyes, yet she felt him drawing her to him as surely as if he'd reached for her with his arms.

The space between them melted away until the distance between his lips and hers could be measured in millimeters. He was so near to her now that she couldn't see him clearly anymore. So she closed her eyes.

Darkness enfolded her as his lips brushed the corner of her mouth. First left, then right. Soft visitations. Misty dreams. This wasn't real, she thought. This wasn't happening. With her eyes shut it was easy to believe it was all a dream.

But the lips grazing hers were warm and very much alive. His mouth tempted but didn't settle. He caressed her lower lip, then skimmed the curve of her upper lip. The pace was slow and inevitable, a seductive build-up.

Once again Brad had taken her by surprise. She hadn't expected this kind of gentleness from him. The intoxicating warmth of his mouth drove her to distraction as he continued his tempting explorations. And then he was finally *really* kissing her. Still he didn't make demands. But by coaxing and teasing, he won her response.

Her lips parted and she swayed closer to him.

And then the rowdy sound of nearby laughter prematurely shattered the moment. Startled, Sabrina pulled away.

She opened her eyes and looked at Brad. Just looked at him. She couldn't seem to get her mind to function yet. She wondered if he was having the same problem. For the time being they both appeared to be speechless.

By mutual, albeit silent, agreement, they left the wharf and headed back to the parking lot. During the short walk, Sabrina strove to marshall her thoughts. By the time they reached her car, she had her speech prepared. It would be back to business as usual. What had happened back there on the wharf was best forgotten. She had no false illusions that Brad had abandoned his grudge against her or changed his way of thinking about her background.

Yes, she was ready to be distant and logical. Brad wasn't. Just as she was about to speak, he put his finger to her lips, stilling her words and her heart.

"I know what you're going to say," he murmured. "Don't." A second later he'd replaced his finger with his lips, kissing her before she could frame a refusal.

Their first kiss had been gentle. This one was hungry. Cupping his hands around her shoulders, he moved closer to her. Sabrina suddenly found herself sandwiched between the unyielding metal of her car door and the equally solid warmth of his very human body.

It was as if they were just picking up where they'd left off at the wharf. The magic was there in a flash and it was as powerful as ever. Her lips parted, granting him access. He explored the inner softness of her mouth with a raw passion that made her weak at the knees. The thrust of his tongue was sensual yet not threatening. It was darkly inviting and she could no more have refused than she could have flown.

Nothing less than the need for oxygen drew them apart this time. As Sabrina came up for air, the enormity of what had just occurred hit her. This time she looked at him with shocked dismay—not at what he'd done, but at the way she'd reacted.

Brad was staring at her with something close to surprise in his eyes, as well. In fact, to Sabrina, he looked pretty darn well stunned. But she couldn't afford to stick around and verify that impression. She had to get out of there while the getting was good.

The fact that she'd forgotten to lock her car saved her. She yanked the door open without needing to use the key she still held in her hand. She closed the door just as quickly. That gave her the moment or two she needed to still the trembling in her fingers so that she could insert said key into the ignition.

Brad's knock on the window made her jump a foot.

She lowered the window a scant inch or two.

"This isn't over," he informed her.

"Yes, it is," she replied.

Then she stepped on the gas and made a speedy if inelegant getaway.

Five

"Okay, what's so important that I had to come down here at eleven at night?" Al demanded as he took the empty bar stool next to Brad. Despite the hour, or perhaps because of it, the tavern was still fairly well populated. Brad had saved him a seat.

"I just thought you might like to have a beer with me, that's all," Brad replied, signaling for the bartender.

"Right. And I'm the King of Siam," said Al.

"If you didn't want to come you should have stayed home, Your Majesty."

"No way! My wife insisted I come get the entire lowdown on what's going on."

"Nothing's going on," Brad denied in a disgruntled tone of voice. "Jeez, can't a man invite his best friend for a beer without the world collapsing?"

"I don't know." Al shrugged good-naturedly. "Why don't *you* tell *me?*"

Brad indicated the beer he'd just paid for. "Drink your beer and be quiet."

"This is the part where I shut up and listen, right? Go ahead," Al magnanimously invited him. "Tell me the whole thing. And don't leave out one titillating detail."

"Now what are you going on about?"

"Come on, buddy, I'm not blind. You've got that glazed look in your eyes. Your mind is definitely somewhere else. On a woman, I'll bet. The one that got away, right? Hey, is she getting to you?"

"Of course not."

"No?"

"No. I've got everything under control."

"Yeah, right."

"What? You don't believe me?"

"All I know is that you just poured pepper in your beer," Al stated.

"I like it that way." And to prove it, Brad took a generous sip.

"Sure you do."

"Al, you're starting to get on my nerves."

"Hey, don't get mad at me because you're having woman trouble."

"I am *not* having woman trouble."

"She's a beautiful lady. She didn't look like she'd be a pushover, though."

"She's not."

"Too bad. Makes it harder, huh? No pun intended."

"You're just a barrel of laughs tonight, aren't you?"

"And you're crabbier than a blind man at a nude beach," Al retorted. "So are you going to tell me what's up or not?"

"I just felt like some company tonight. Any crime in that?"

"No crime at all. That's what buddies are for."

"Well then..." Brad clinked his glass against Al's. "To good friends."

"To good friends," Al echoed. "And to the one that got away."

She'd gotten away again tonight, Brad thought to himself. She'd tempted him and then taken off. But he could handle it. Like he'd told Al, he was still in control.

Then why did you call Al? a taunting voice in his head mocked him. Why are you sitting here eating stale peanuts and drinking peppery beer? Because you can't be where you want to be...in bed with Sabrina. Or because that kiss shook you so damn much you had to call in reinforcements. Take your pick.

"We went out to dinner tonight," Brad heard himself admitting.

"No kidding? Congratulations. You must be doing a good job of reeling her in. What's your next move?"

Brad shifted uneasily. Suddenly his old plans no longer felt comfortable—like shoes that had shrunk in the rain. "I haven't decided yet," he hedged.

What had started out for him as a means of revenge had turned into a source of extreme frustration. And extreme excitement. One thing hadn't changed however. Brad still wanted Sabrina Stewart—now more than ever!

"You want more?" Sabrina asked her cat Thomas, who'd already devoured two slices of roast beef. "You must have a hollow leg."

At least her own legs had regained their steadiness, Sabrina noted. She'd still been shaky when she'd gotten home. The phrase *I can't believe I did that!* kept replaying in her mind.

"I should know better," Sabrina told herself as she gave the cat the last bit of beef. "I knew what Brad was after from the start. But I didn't know I'd like it so much when he kissed me," she muttered. "I need to have my head examined. Maybe there was something in those fried clams. Or the turtle sundae. Maybe I can chalk it up to temporary insanity. Whatever it was, it can't happen again."

Thomas yodeled his agreement.

"You should have seen me. I went as limp as a dishrag. Powerless to resist. I don't know where my backbone went."

Sabrina dug out a new bag of cheese curls and took it back to the living room couch with her. That and a classic Jimmy Stewart movie were her intended cure for whatever ailed her. She'd already vacuumed the living room rug—twice—and since it was after eleven she doubted her downstairs neighbors had appreciated her sudden cleaning frenzy. She'd also separated her recyclable items into their appropriate bins. Then she'd bicycled half a mile on her exercise bike, which hadn't helped the stability of her legs any.

Now she was stretched out, determined to put her mind on hold and relax so she could get some sleep. An empty bag of cheese curls later, she was still remembering the feel of Brad's lips on hers. He was not an easy man to forget.

And to make things worse, the next morning she had an appointment with his grandparents. She just prayed he wouldn't be there. She needed a little more time to get herself together again. Just a little more time. Then she'd be fine.

On that note, Sabrina fell asleep.

Sabrina's appointment with Brad's grandparents took longer than she'd expected. The fault was Joseph's. He was a great storyteller; he just didn't know when to stop.

Of course it didn't help that Sabrina had a headache caused by a crick in her neck—a souvenir left from spending half the night on the couch. The dull pain made it harder to concentrate.

"That's very interesting, Joseph," she said, having been told by the older man to call him by his first name. *Mr. Romanovski is my son's name,* he'd told her. "But I think it's time we talked about Violet. Tell me about *your* childhood," Sabrina invited her.

"There's not much to tell. I was only seventeen when we got married," Violet said.

"So was I," Joseph interjected. "We both had to ask our parents' permission to get married."

"They gave it, of course," Violet continued, "although my parents were a little hesitant at first."

"Her father never liked me. He worked for the post office. Do we have to include him in this video?"

"We're not cutting out my father just because you didn't get along with him," Violet declared indignantly.

"Fine. We'll have him in then. But if he's in, so is my Uncle Luigi."

"He's not even your real uncle!"

"We can work out those details later," Sabrina hastily inserted. "Maybe you two could tell me about the first time you met?"

"It was in August..." Violet began.

"It was late July," Joseph corrected her. "I remember distinctly because it was right after my mother's birthday."

"Anyway, I was walking down the street..."

"She was actually on the sidewalk," Joseph said.

Exasperated, Violet said, "Who's telling this story, you or me?"

"No need to get so touchy about it. I was just trying to be helpful. We want to make sure all the facts are correct, don't we?"

"Go on, Violet," Sabrina prompted.

"I was on my way to a birthday party for a friend of mine—"

"Shirley MacCalley," Joseph added. "She moved to Indiana two years after that."

"When I met Joseph here, who was also heading for the same party."

"I knew her brother," Joseph inserted. "We used to play hooky from school together."

"You knew Violet's brother?" Sabrina asked.

"No," Joseph replied. "Shirley's brother. Bob."

"Then what happened?" Sabrina quickly inquired, before Joseph went off on a tangent about Shirley and her brother Bob. She'd learned that to keep him on track you had to head him off at the pass, so to speak.

"I walked her to the front door," Joseph said. "We hit it off right away."

"Is that right?" Sabrina asked Violet, wanting to hear her side of the story.

"Actually, I thought he was awfully forward at first."

"I had to be forward," Joseph defended himself. "There was a war on!"

"The war didn't start until 1941," Violet reminded him. "By then Joe Junior was born."

"Well, I knew the war was coming. Everybody knew it."

The look Violet gave Sabrina said otherwise, but the woman held her tongue.

"Anyway, I swept her off her feet and two months later we were married," Joseph proudly declared.

"A year after that Brad's father, Joe Junior, was born," Violet added.

"Then the war came, but I already told you about my time in the U.S. Navy," Joseph said.

He certainly had.

"And this photograph is of your mother?" Sabrina asked Joseph, wanting to make sure she had that correct.

"That's right. It was her idea that we come to this country from Poland. She was a widow with a young boy to raise and she thought we could have a better life here. I can still remember being in New York City and the excitement I felt. One day we went up the Chrysler Building and I thought I was on top of the world. But the thing that sticks in my mind the most from those early days was my first taste of chewing gum. I couldn't believe this stuff that you chewed but didn't swallow or eat. Who could make sense of that?"

"There are a lot of things you can't make sense of," Sabrina agreed, knowing her attraction to Brad was one of them.

When Brad came to Memories later that day to view the remainder of the family's video tape, Sabrina was ready for him. She'd spent the better part of the previous hour mentally preparing herself. Outwardly she'd been editing the Friedman wedding tape, but inwardly she'd been lecturing herself. She was not going to let Brad get to her again.

He was doing it on purpose. She had no doubt of that. Maybe it was his way of getting back at her for whatever offenses he imagined she'd committed against him when they'd been teenagers. Maybe getting her to fall for him was a way he could get back at her.

Or maybe she simply presented a challenge to him. She didn't know for sure. She only knew that getting involved with Brad was definitely not a wise move.

The incident on the wharf last night had also taught her that she wasn't safe around him, regardless of how long her skirt was! So she'd made a point of wearing slacks today. Baggy navy-blue ones. Not the least bit sexy. Her outfit was practical yet still fashionable, the cropped white sweater with its navy piping adding a nice nautical touch.

She'd only spent a few minutes checking her appearance in the mirror, just long enough to make sure that her hair hadn't come undone from the white bow she'd fastened it with. The style, gathered away from her face with the sides loosely twisted and then held in place with a touch of hair spray, suited her intended mood—at ease and in control.

At least she *looked* as if she were in charge of things, including her wayward emotions. That was half the battle won right there. Now she just had to win the war.

It wouldn't be easy. No doubt Brad planned on pulling out all the stops this evening, making the most of their unavoidably close proximity in the viewing room. Sabrina resolutely reminded herself that she'd handled passes from clients before with no difficulty. But then no client had ever affected her the way Brad did and continued to do. This kind of thing had never been a problem before.

"And it won't be a problem now," she told herself.

"Talking to yourself? Not a good sign," Brad murmured from behind her.

Damn it, he'd crept up on her!

"The girl at the desk out there told me to come on in," he added.

Sabrina would have the new girl's head on a platter! Unfortunately there weren't enough employees at Memories that they could afford to lose one. Counting Eliot, there were only four of them working full-time, with two more part-timers on the roster. Still, visitors were always supposed to be announced, especially this visitor.

"You seem upset," Brad noted dryly. "Something wrong?"

"It's just been a long day, that's all." That much was true. Aside from interviewing Brad's grandparents that morning, she'd also had to deal with Guy Smythe-Jones—who'd lived up to his reputation as a playboy by demanding plenty of what he called "personal attention," with the emphasis on *personal*.

She'd kept one step ahead of him, no problem, but it had lengthened the shoot of the restoration work he'd done on the family mansion by another hour. Some people wanted a chronicle of their family. Guy wanted a chronicle of his belongings!

Sabrina hadn't known him very well when she'd spent her summers here—a deliberate omission on her part. Brad might have intimidated her when she'd been younger, but

Guy had given her the willies. The blond-haired, blue-eyed prince of society was no Prince Charming in her book.

Neither is Brad, she sternly reminded herself. Yes, but he's head and shoulders above Guy, a taunting voice inside her head insisted. She couldn't argue that point.

"If you're ready," she briskly stated, "we can look at the rest of the video tape now and get that over with."

"You're in a hurry all of a sudden."

"It's just that it's already been a long..."

"A long day. I know." It had been a long day for him, too, one spent brooding about the kisses they'd shared the night before. She'd come alive in his arms, exceeding even his wildest expectations. Much as Brad told himself he had things under control, deep down he knew that wasn't the case. He also knew that he had to touch her again or he'd go nuts.

She wasn't going to make it easy for him. He could tell that she'd retreated into her ivory tower again. He'd just have to coax her back out of it.

To that end, he made sure that his hand brushed hers when she handed him the sheet of scenes they'd agreed on yesterday. And the longer they sat beside each other, the more the tension and the awareness between them increased.

A stolen touch here, a wicked look there, and Sabrina's hard-fought-for composure was ready to snap. The way he was presently studying her mouth instead of the TV monitor was the last straw.

"This can't continue," she exclaimed. "I know what you're up to!"

"Oh? And what am I up to?"

"No good."

"Oh, but it was good last night, wasn't it?" he said softly. "Incredibly good. And that's what's got you scared."

She got up and paced. "I am not scared. Disconcerted and uneasy, maybe. But not scared."

"What have you got to be uneasy about?"

"Your motives, let alone your intentions."

"Are you asking me what my intentions are?"

"Of course not." Put that way it sounded as if she was trying to trap him into making some kind of commitment to her. "I'm just saying that I don't want any complications."

"Neither do I. So why are you being difficult about this?"

"Because I don't know what *this* is!"

"It's attraction. Pure and simple."

"For you maybe. There's nothing simple about it for me. If you've got some kind of hidden agenda going here, I want to know about it."

"Are you speaking figuratively again?"

"Come on, Brad. I know how you feel about me. You've made that clear enough since I've returned to Newport. You thought I was a spoiled rich kid and maybe you see this as your chance to get back at me."

Brad shifted uncomfortably at having his original intentions so easily pegged.

"Or maybe it's that Romanovski family rule of yours," she continued. "Someone tells you that you can't and you make a point of proving them wrong."

"You think this is a game with me?"

"You said yourself that some games get better as you grow older. And that you planned on teaching me that."

"That was before..."

"Before what?"

Before I knew your kisses could drive me around the bend. Make me go off the deep end. Keep me awake nights. The words went through his mind, but he didn't speak them aloud. He didn't want her knowing the hold she was beginning to have on him.

"Before I got to know you better," he said.

"And now you don't think I was spoiled as a teenager?"

"I wouldn't go that far."

"We're not going far together at all," she stated. "Because I don't want to play any more games with you."

"Oh, you want to play, all right. You're just..."

"Don't you dare accuse me of being afraid again!"

"Is that why you never learned how to swim? Because you're afraid?"

"I am not afraid of either you or the water!" she denied. "I never learned how to swim because I never got around to it and there wasn't anyone handy to teach me."

"That's easy to fix. You've got the time now and someone to show you how. I'll teach you how to swim. Now. Tonight."

"Are you crazy?"

"Not at all. My apartment complex has a pool that's open at night. I can't promise you'll learn how to swim by the end of the evening, but at least you'll have had the first lesson."

"No, I won't. I have no intention of getting into a pool with you."

"You prefer the ocean?"

"You are not teaching me how to swim," she unequivocally stated.

"You don't trust me?"

"You've got that right!"

"Think I'll try and take advantage of you in your skimpy little swimsuit?"

"I do not own a skimpy little swimsuit."

"Pity. Look, I'll make a deal with you. How about I promise to be on my best behavior if you'll let me teach you how to swim?"

"Forget it."

"In that case, I guess I can do this—" he sauntered over and placed a series of tiny kisses along the column of her throat "—as often as I want to."

"No, you can't!" She jumped away from him as if he were the devil and she were trying to avoid temptation, which wasn't far from the truth. "Whatever gives you that idea?"

"Because you obviously don't want me to be on my best behavior, otherwise you would have agreed to my offer."

"Correction. I obviously don't want you to teach me how to swim. And I refuse to be baited into letting you try."

"You can be incredibly stubborn," he said in exasperation. "Do you know that?"

"I'm not trying to challenge you, Brad," she quietly informed him. "There's a difference between *can't* and *don't*. I *don't* want you to teach me how to swim. You're not going to get anywhere on that front."

"And what about this front?" He trailed his finger over her parted lips.

"Careful." She gently but firmly nipped his finger with her teeth. "You might get more than you bargained for!"

Brad just smiled. "I'm counting on it."

"The only thing I'm counting on is finishing this video tonight," she said briskly. "Let's get back to work."

Sabrina didn't see either Brad or his grandparents again until the following Tuesday, for which she was infinitely grateful. The four-day break helped her regain some of her former equilibrium. She'd tangled with Brad and managed to hold her own. Surely that made up for the momentary weakness of melting in his arms that one night they'd kissed?

"Are you getting this on that tape machine of yours?" Joseph asked her, interrupting her thoughts—which still had a frustrating tendency to focus on Brad.

Sabrina checked the recorder. Thank heavens it was still on record. "Yes, it's fine. Go on. You were telling me about the early years of your marriage."

"Well, as I was saying, I was working down at the boat yards then. Violet was home with the three kids."

"Holding down the fort," Violet added, the first time she'd spoken in the past twenty minutes. "In those days a woman was expected to stay home. You girls nowadays have got it good. You can do whatever you want to do, be whatever you want to be."

"But a lot of women today have a double burden of going out to work while *still* being responsible for the same duties you had of raising the children, cooking the meals and keeping the house," Sabrina pointed out.

"I wouldn't have minded staying home and taking care of the kids instead of working fourteen-hour days," Joseph stated.

"My job was no piece of cake," Violet informed him. "You've never appreciated the work I put in—making a paycheck stretch, managing the household accounts, keeping the kids out of your hair so you could concentrate on work."

"I never said you didn't have a good head on your shoulders."

"You never said anything!"

"You've been my wife almost fifty years. You should know these things by now," Joseph said in a dismissive tone of voice.

Watching Violet's face turn red, Sabrina experienced a sudden sinking feeling—an internal premonition of trouble. Surely these two weren't about to fight, were they?

"I had dreams, too, you know," Violet said. "I wanted to paint!"

"So who stopped you?"

"You did. Whenever I picked up a paint brush you made fun of me."

"That didn't stop you. You went out and took those lessons from the community center even though I asked you not to."

"You *told* me not to." Violet turned to face Sabrina. "And do you know why? Because it would mean that I would be out of the house on Monday and Wednesday nights and he didn't want to make supper for himself. I even said I'd leave it in the fridge for him, but no. He didn't like that idea one bit."

"If you want to neglect your duties..." Joseph began.

"I wanted to get out two nights a week!" Violet retorted. "You've always gone out bowling every Friday night."

"Then you should have taken painting lessons on Friday night when I was out."

"They didn't offer them Friday night."

By now their voices had risen to a shout. Sabrina eyed them both in consternation. "Yes, well, maybe we should talk about something else..."

"And another thing," Joseph went on to say, completely ignoring Sabrina. "You're always correcting me whenever I'm talking."

"You're the one who does that," Violet protested. "Not me. *You* always interrupt *me*..."

"I do not!"

"Like you did just now. You never listen to me."

"I don't know what you're talking about. Here, give me the remote control. The Cubs game is starting."

"I've had forty-nine years of you turning me off and turning the TV on. I've had it, Joseph. It's time you got your priorities straight. And it's time you started appreciating me, which means respecting the things that are important to me."

"Do you respect what's important to me? If you did you wouldn't start an argument while I'm trying to watch the game."

"You'll be able to watch the game in peace," Violet assured him.

"Good."

"And all the rest of the games in peace. Because I'm leaving!"

"Going shopping? We're out of pretzels."

"No. I'm not going shopping. I'm going to pack! I'm not staying here a minute longer!"

"Brad, Sabrina is on line one," his secretary told him. "She sounds upset."

Brad punched the appropriate phone button. "What's up?"

"You might want to get over here," Sabrina said.

"Is something wrong?" he demanded. "Are my grandparents okay? Was there an accident?"

"No, no. Nothing like that."

"Then what's wrong? Is there some problem with the interview?"

"You could say that. Your grandmother is packing."

"Packing?" Brad repeated in disbelief. "Why?"

"She says she's leaving your grandfather and she's talking about moving in with you!"

Six

"What's going on here?" Brad demanded as he entered his grandparent's house.

"Oh, there you are, Bradley," his grandmother said. "Good. You can carry these bags out to your car. You did say you had an extra bedroom at your apartment, didn't you?"

"Yes, but—"

"Good. I knew I could count on you to be thoughtful and supportive, unlike some members of the male population." Violet threw a meaningful glare in Joseph's direction.

Sabrina noted that Joseph didn't even look away from the Cubs game he was still watching.

"I'll wait for you in the car, Bradley," Violet stated emphatically.

"I'll go out with you," Sabrina hurriedly offered, deciding it might be wise to leave the two men alone together to talk.

Brad closed the front door after the two women and turned to face his grandfather. "Okay, why don't you tell me what's going on here?"

"The bases were loaded when their shortstop, with a count of zero and two, hit a round-tripper that really cleaned the bases."

"I'm not talking about the game." Brad walked over and turned the sound down. "Now tell me, what's going on between you and Grandma?"

Joseph shrugged. "Your grandmother has gone off the deep end. Must be her hormones or something."

"But you two never fight."

"We didn't fight this time, either. She just upped and packed her bag. I don't know what's the matter with her. She says I don't pay any attention to her. Can you believe that? Told me she wants to leave. She went on and on about how she wants to paint. I'm telling you, it must be hormones. Your grandmother's never carried on so."

Trying to reassure his grandfather, Brad said, "She'll calm down in an hour or two, I'm sure." I hope! he added mentally.

"I'm sure she will. Maybe you should take her out to lunch or something—you know, to make her feel better."

"Sure thing. And don't you worry. This will blow over by tonight."

But after he'd picked up his grandmother's bags and gone out to talk to her and Sabrina, Brad wasn't so sure about things quickly blowing over. His grandmother looked mad enough to spit cotton while Sabrina stood by, looking gorgeous but worried.

"Impossible man!" Violet was muttering from the passenger seat of his car. "I've had it with his correcting me every two seconds. What does he think I am, stupid? I've just had it with him!"

Taking Sabrina by the elbow, Brad pulled her aside so that they wouldn't be overheard. "What the hell happened here?"

"They had a fight."

"No kidding," he noted sarcastically. "I would never have guessed. I mean specifically. Tell me *exactly* what happened."

"Your grandfather kept interrupting your grandmother time after time, disagreeing or correcting what she said, and I guess she got tired of it."

He frowned. "That's it? Because of that she's packed her bags and leaving him after fifty years of marriage?"

"They're *your* grandparents," she pointed out. "You know them better than I do."

"I thought I did."

"What are you going to do?"

"Take my grandmother out to lunch and hope she calms down."

"I don't think a lunch is going to be enough," Sabrina said. "She's quite upset."

"I can't believe this is happening. They never fight. Are you sure you didn't say something... ?"

Sabrina couldn't blame him for asking that question. She'd been asking it of herself as well. "All I was doing was interviewing them about how they met and that sort of thing. Somehow they got onto the subject of your grandmother taking painting classes and your grandfather disapproving. Things escalated pretty fast after that and then Joseph just turned on the Cubs game and ignored her."

Brad shook his head in confusion. "Granddad's always watching a game. That's nothing new."

"Perhaps your grandmother had simply had it with being taken for granted. The woman has spent her life taking care of her family. She's got a right to expect some emotional support back from that family."

"Of course she does. And I'll do what I can, but I'm no expert at this." He restlessly speared his fingers through his dark hair, before admitting, "My sister's much better at handling family crises than I am. Wouldn't you know that she'd be vacationing in Cancun at a time like this. She always did have lousy timing."

"Is there a problem, Bradley?" Violet called out the car window. "You haven't put my bags in the car yet."

"No. No problem. I'll be right there." Turning to Sabrina, he said, "I'll call you later."

"Please do."

For the rest of the afternoon Sabrina couldn't shake the feeling that she was somehow to blame for the flare-up between the older Romanovskis. After all, they had been married all those years and managed not to fight. Then along she came, and suddenly all hell broke loose!

The incident only served to reinforce Sabrina's doubts—her Achilles' heel. Perhaps if she'd had more experience with family relationships she might have been able to do something to prevent the argument from escalating out of control the way it had. Instead she'd just sat there like a spectator at a tennis match, watching the verbal volleys going back and forth between Violet and Joseph, yet unable to intervene.

Maybe she was jinxed where families were concerned, she thought. Heaven knew that her own relationship with her family was on the distant side, though not through any choice of her own. That's simply the way her parents were. Distant. Unable to relate on an emotional level. And they'd passed that trait on to their daughter.

Her parents were passionate in their dedication to protecting the planet. However, they did not have a similarly passionate dedication to parenthood. Outward displays of affection were frowned upon, so as a child Sabrina hadn't received any hugs or much encouragement.

When Sabrina had preferred history and the fine arts over science in high school, she could still remember the way her parents had looked at her with bewildered dismay—as if wondering if they'd mistakenly been given the wrong baby at the hospital. While she could share their deep concern about the planet, she couldn't share their increasingly single-minded fervor. She couldn't live up to their expectations, and they wouldn't change those expectations to suit her needs.

Now that Sabrina was an adult, her parents were still unable to relate to her. She knew they were especially dissatisfied with her choice of career. They couldn't understand why anyone would want to do something as frivolous as videotaping weddings or compiling video tapes of family histories. Didn't she realize the hole in the earth's ozone layer was growing by the day? She should at least be working on documentaries about that, or the fate of the dolphins, or the disastrous effect of oil spills.

It didn't matter that she contributed to organizations that did focus on those problems. It didn't matter that she recycled. It was never enough.

In the end, Sabrina had given up trying to please her parents regarding her job and life-style. Now she pleased herself. Or tried to. But this feeling of inadequacy still haunted her sometimes. At the moment it felt particularly strong.

So it was with nervous dread that she waited for Brad's call that evening. The news was not good.

"My grandmother has taken up residence in my spare room and she's not showing any sign of being the least bit homesick," he told her. "In fact, she seems to be having a great time."

Brad sounded so rattled that she felt sorry for him. "How are you holding up?"

"I'm not. The damn phone's been ringing off the hook. My grandfather called, wanting to know when she's coming home to cook his dinner. She refused to speak to him.

So then my grandfather called my parents, who called me. My dad's siding with my grandfather, my mom with my grandmother. This thing's turned into a regular battle of the sexes and I'm right in the middle of it," he said in exasperation. "I ended up having to come out here to use my car phone so that I could speak without my grandmother overhearing me."

This was sounding even worse than she'd expected. "Is there anything I can do?"

"We've got to get them back together again. I know they love each other. They just need some coaxing."

"You're usually pretty good at that."

"So are you. Which means that if we work together we should be able to get them together again."

"What do you suggest we do?" she asked.

"I don't know. I was hoping you'd have a suggestion."

"Well, how about we start by just talking to them? Since you said this has turned into a battle of the sexes, then maybe it would be best if I spoke to your grandmother and you spoke to your grandfather. You know, sort of woman-to-woman, man-to-man, that sort of thing. Remind them what it is they love about each other, how much they mean to each other."

"It's worth a try. Surely it can't get worse than it already is."

"Let's hope not."

"When do you think you can talk to my grandmother?"

"I'll talk to her tomorrow right after work," Sabrina said.

"That would be great. Come on over to my place. While you're here, I'll be over at their house trying to talk to my grandfather."

"Sounds like a plan."

"Yes, it does. And Sabrina..."

"Yes?"

"Thanks."

She cradled the receiver against her ear, savoring the gentleness of his voice. "That's okay," she said somewhat awkwardly. "I'll do whatever I can to help."

But after she'd hung up, Sabrina wondered who would help *her*. Because she had a sinking feeing that the more time she spent with Brad and his family, the more vulnerable she was becoming. And that was not a good thing, not where a man like Brad was concerned.

As she had promised, Sabrina headed straight for Brad's apartment right after work. He'd faxed her a map with directions that were as detailed as the last one he'd drawn for her. The building was much newer and a great deal more luxurious than her own. The location was better, too.

His grandmother opened the door for her. "Brad had some last-minute work to do. He told me you two were going out to dinner tonight and that I was to keep you occupied until he gets here."

Oh, he did, did he? Sabrina thought to herself. She had no intention of going out to dinner with him. At least not alone. Look what had happened the last time they'd done that. He'd kissed her until she couldn't think straight. She sure hoped he didn't plan on using this opportunity to try to make another move on her.

"He invited me to come along," Violet added, lessening Sabrina's fears somewhat, "but I told him I didn't want to get in the way."

"You wouldn't be in the way. In fact, it wouldn't be the same without you. You should definitely join us." Because if you don't, I'm not going, she added to herself.

"I'll think about it," Violet said. "Meanwhile come on in and sit down. You'll have to excuse the somewhat wild decorating. My granddaughter is an interior decorator and she practiced on Brad's living room. She claimed it's an example of her black and white period."

It certainly was. The walls were white, the furniture black. Very stark. Even the large painting hanging over the black leather couch was a geometric design in black and white.

"Brad tells me he's going to do it over himself as soon as he gets the time. He says he feels like he's color blind when he's in this room. But then he's probably already told you that himself. No? Well no doubt you two have other things you talk about."

Or argue about, Sabrina thought to herself. But her relationship with Brad was not the center of conversation here, at least it wasn't meant to be. Somehow she had to get Violet to talk about herself and her relationship with Joseph.

"Can I get you something to drink while you're waiting?" Violet asked.

"No, thanks. So, how have you been doing?" Subtle, she thought to herself in disgust. Real subtle. She'd majored in communications in college. You'd think that would include verbal as well as visual communications.

"I'm fine. The mattress on Brad's extra bed is very comfortable. And there's no snoring to keep me awake. Joseph snores, you know." Violet paused a moment before admitting, "One or two times in the night I did get lonely—"

Aha, Sabrina thought to herself. Now we're getting somewhere!

"But I just hugged a pillow and fell right back to sleep again," Violet said cheerfully. "I even did some sketching today. And I started a watercolor. Would you like to see it?"

"Sure." She took the artist's pad that Violet handed her. "Why, it's the Old Stone Mill in Touro Park."

"You recognize it." The older woman sounded very pleased.

"Of course I do. You've captured it exactly. The roughness of the stone, the curve of the arches. You've even managed to get the perspective just right to convey the round shape of the building. This is wonderful!"

"You're too kind," Violet murmured.

"No, I mean it. You're very talented."

"You really think so?"

"Absolutely," Sabrina replied.

Violet beamed. "I'm so glad you think so. After everything that Joseph's said to me over the years I began wondering if I had any talent at all. He'd tease me and call them my scribbles." Her smile faded. "Whenever we went to Touro Park and I tried to sketch the mill, Joseph would keep interrupting me—telling me about all the mysteries of the building's origins. Not only that, but each time we visited it, he'd change his mind about what he'd believe. One time he'd agree that it was the ruins of a Norse church dating back nine hundred years. The next visit he'd decide it was really the ruin of a windmill built by one of our state's early governors, I forget which one." Violet rolled her vivid blue eyes in exasperation. "I didn't care about the historical origins of the mill, I was just trying to sketch it! You need to concentrate when you're drawing. But Joseph was a constant distraction."

Sabrina nodded understandingly. She knew someone else who was a real distraction. Brad. He made her think about him when she should be concentrating on something else, her work, or even the laundry. She'd already botched an editing job that had taken another hour to redo—and she'd ruined one of her favorite white blouses by throwing a red shirt in with it by mistake.

To be fair, he hadn't been actually present while she'd made those mistakes. He'd certainly been in her mind, however. But who was to blame for that? Him or her? It was a frustrating situation.

Violet patted her hand. "You look like you know what I'm talking about. Has my grandson done the same thing to you?"

"Not exactly the same thing, no. I guess the Romanovski men are just distracting in one way or another. Maybe it's a family trait? I haven't met Brad's father yet. Is he distracting, too?"

"Oh, no. Joe Junior is very easygoing. But yes, I do believe you're right. It is a family trait. It's just skipped a generation. It's made life much easier for my daughter-in-law, I can tell you. She doesn't have to deal with the things I do. Joe Junior is very attentive. They got married when they were very young, too. When Brad's mother called me today, she was very supportive. Said it was about time Joseph started appreciating me."

"Maybe he just needs some lessons on how to do that," Sabrina suggested.

"The man's almost seventy. If he hasn't learned by now, I don't know if there's much hope of him ever learning."

"After all you've put into your marriage, you shouldn't give up so easily now, Violet. You're a smart woman. Surely there's a way you can teach Joseph what he needs to know."

"I've tried talking to him. He nods but he doesn't really listen. He hears me all right. He can repeat verbatim every word I said, but the meaning doesn't sink in with him. Do you know what I mean?"

Sabrina nodded. Unfortunately both her parents suffered from the same problem themselves. But she sensed greater potential within Joseph. She judged him to be a man of deep emotions.

"Has Joseph always had trouble expressing his emotions?" Sabrina asked.

"Not at all. Usually you knew exactly what he was feeling. He'd show it right away. You could tell if he was happy or angry. It's only been lately that he's become so...I don't know. So unresponsive. It's so hard to have a conversation with him these days. Even when he's not watching TV he's so intent on keeping the attention focused on himself that you can't get any sort of discussion going. We used to talk about things all the time. Now whatever I say, he says 'I knew that.' It's like we're suddenly in some kind of competition together. And it wears you out, I can tell you."

Sabrina nodded understandingly.

Violet sighed. "Maybe I spoiled him. He got too used to having his own way. He didn't even see me anymore. Not as a separate person. A person with interests of my own."

"And talent," Sabrina added, holding up the pad she still held.

"You really think I'm good?"

"Yes, I do. Have you shown Brad this painting?"

"Not yet. I'm not sure he'd be interested," Violet confessed.

"I'm sure he would be." And if he wasn't she'd personally slug him herself! Violet had a wonderful gift and she should be encouraged by her family to cultivate that talent, not held back.

"Have you ever shown Joseph your work?" Sabrina asked.

"He's seen some of it, but he didn't seem the least bit interested so I didn't bother showing him again."

"Maybe you need to give him another chance. Maybe if he saw how good you are, he'd see things differently."

In Middletown, Brad was sharing a beer with his grandfather, trying to steer the conversation away from baseball and onto the matter at hand.

"I suppose your grandmother sent you over here," Joseph said.

Brad wasn't sure how to answer that one. Should he deny it and hurt his grandfather's feelings? Or agree and give him a false sense of security? "She's pretty mad, Granddad. I don't think this is just a little thing for her."

"It's not a little thing for me, either! I had to eat pizza last night. There was no dinner. Your dad brought it over for me. The two of us had a good time, though. You know, we should plan more men-only nights," Joseph suggested thoughtfully.

Brad began to panic. "You wouldn't want all your nights to be like last night, though, would you?"

"Of course not."

Thank heavens. Now he was finally getting somewhere, Brad thought to himself.

"You know how I hate pizza," Joseph added.

Frustrated, Brad turned the TV off. He couldn't concentrate with that thing going. "We need to talk. You love Grandma, don't you?"

"What kind of stupid question is that?" he countered irritably. "Of course, I do. I've been married to the woman for almost fifty years. She knows how I feel about her."

"Does she? When was the last time you told her?"

"I don't know. It wasn't that long ago."

Brad persisted. "When exactly was it? Think about it."

"I know." Joseph snapped his fingers triumphantly. "It was right before that fancy party your sister threw to celebrate her new job."

"That was over a year ago."

"It couldn't have been. Was it that long? Really?"

Brad nodded.

"I didn't realize," Joseph said slowly.

"It's not too late, you know. You could come over to my place right now and tell her you love her. Or phone her." Brad reached for the phone.

"Now hold on, there. Why should I be the one phoning her? She walked out on me."

For the first time Brad saw the hurt his grandfather was experiencing. He placed a consoling hand on the older man's shoulder. "You should be the one to call her because you're man enough to make the first step."

"All right. Maybe I will call her, but I'm not going to apologize. Not right off, not until she does."

"Just call her."

* * *

"Do you want me to answer the phone?" Sabrina asked Violet after it had rung twice and the other woman showed no signs of getting up.

"No, that's all right, dear. Brad has one of those complicated newfangled answering machines hooked up to it and I'm afraid of messing things up if I answer it."

"What if it's Brad calling?"

"Then he can leave a message. He's got it set so that I can hear whoever leaves the message."

But after the sound of the beep there was only the buzz of the dial tone. "They hung up," Violet said with a shrug. "Must have been someone selling something."

"She's not there," Joseph said. "I just got that newfangled answering machine of yours. Stupid contraption."

"She's there. She just didn't pick up the phone. I'll call her."

"If she's there maybe it would better if I spoke to her face-to-face," Joseph said.

"You're right," Brad agreed. "That would be best."

But as Brad stood in his living room, watching the cool looks passing between his grandparents, he wondered if this had been such a good idea after all.

"You didn't tell me you were bringing your grandfather home with you, Bradley."

"It wasn't my idea," Joseph stated belligerently.

"Why don't we all sit down," Brad suggested. As he sat on the couch next to Sabrina he noticed something on the normally bare, black lacquer coffee table. "What's this?"

"Your grandmother painted that this afternoon," Sabrina replied.

"Hey, this is the Old Stone Mill, isn't it?" Brad asked.

Violet nodded and looked so uncertain that Sabrina wanted to nudge Brad into saying something reassuring to her. But to her relief he did so without any prompting from her. "This is great! I'd like to put this on my wall in the office. Would you mind?"

"Not at all," Violet replied. "It's not that good, but if you like it..."

"What do you mean, 'not that good'? I told you, this is great! I had no idea..." Brad's voice drifted off as he realized he'd never taken the time to inquire about her artwork before. He vaguely remembered her taking lessons but had never paid another thought to the matter. "Look, Granddad, isn't this great?" He held it up for Joseph's perusal.

"You know that they still aren't sure who actually built that tower," Joseph informed them. "Some people call it the oldest structure in America, but the experts have yet to come up with any definite evidence to explain the mill's true origin."

Sabrina almost rolled her eyes. Joseph was at it again. Turning the conversation away from the painting and onto himself and his knowledge of the area.

"What?" Joseph demanded, having apparently noticed the disapproval of everyone else in the room. "Now what did I say?"

"The wrong thing, as usual," Violet retorted. "You could have said how you liked the painting. You could have said whether it was good or not."

"Well, of course it's good," Joseph retorted. "I figure you know you're good without me telling you."

"And how am I supposed to know that?"

"Because any fool idiot can see that you've got talent!" Joseph shouted. "That doesn't mean I have to dwell on it. Because if I do—" he lowered his voice before continuing "—maybe you'll leave me to go off painting."

"Oh, Joseph. I wish you'd told me this before," Violet murmured.

The older man's face brightened. "Does this mean you're ready to come home now?"

"It means I'm more likely to consider it, yes."

"Consider it?" He frowned. "What kind of talk is that? A woman's place is at home!"

"In front of the stove, and not an artist's easel, right?" Violet added.

"One's got nothing to do with the other," Joseph protested.

"Yes, it does. You know, since you've retired, you've got more free time to do the things you want to do—bowl, watch baseball games, putter in the garden. But I haven't gotten to retire. I still have to do the same things I was doing before you retired—all the cooking, cleaning and washing. Only now, I get to do those things with you watching me every step of the way, hanging over my shoulder and telling me that I'm overboiling the vegetables or using too much laundry detergent."

"I was just trying to be helpful," Joseph protested.

"You want to be helpful, *you* do the wash," Violet retorted. "Or cook dinner. Or take me out for a meal every other night. It doesn't have to be fancy, just as long as I don't have to cook."

"But I thought you liked to cook."

"I do. But I've been doing it for almost fifty years now," Violet pointed out. "I could use a break."

"Why didn't you ever tell me this before?" Joseph asked.

"I've tried. You wouldn't listen."

"I suppose we could go out to dinner a little more often," he acknowledged.

"Good." Violet nodded her approval. "We'll start tonight."

"You mean you'll move back home tonight?" Joseph said.

"No. I mean we'll go out to dinner tonight. With Brad and Sabrina."

Joseph gave a dismissive shake of his head. "They don't want us old fogies with them."

"Yes, we do," Sabrina quickly assured him. The look she gave Brad told him he'd better agree with her, which he did.

"Sure, Granddad. Come along with us."

"Maybe they could give us some pointers on how modern relationships work," Violet suggested mischievously.

"And maybe we could teach them a thing or two, as well," Joseph added. "Okay." He nodded his agreement. "And after dinner, you'll come home," he stated firmly.

But Violet just smiled sweetly and said, "We'll see."

Seven

The restaurant Brad chose was casual yet romantic, with fresh flowers and flickering candles set out on checked tablecloths. The place also had one of the best ocean views in town. The fact that Brad installed a security system for the owner's cabin cruiser was the only thing that had gotten him a window-side table on such short notice.

He'd planned on coming here with Sabrina to celebrate the success of their joint effort to get his grandparents back together again. Instead here he was—part of a foursome. Not exactly what he'd had in mind when he'd made the reservation.

"You know, I haven't been here in ages," Violet was saying.

"We were here four years ago," Joseph promptly reminded her. "On Labor Day."

Sabrina shook her head. Joseph, bless his obtuse soul, was at it again, correcting his wife over the smallest detail. Recognizing the warning signs of Violet's anger, she tried to head off trouble by distracting the other woman. "What are you going to have?" Sabrina asked her.

"No crab," Violet stated with a meaningful look in Joseph's direction. "I've had enough of crab lately."

Joseph just frowned in confusion. "We haven't had crab since last March."

"I wasn't referring to seafood," Violet retorted.

Brad looked from his grandmother to his grandfather and hastily ordered a beer. This evening could still be trickier than he had thought.

"I'll have the lobster thermidor," Violet decided.

"It's the most expensive thing on the menu," Joseph protested. Seeing the look in his wife's eye he wisely backed down. "But it does sound good. I'll have that, as well."

"Dinner's on me tonight, Granddad," Brad inserted. "Don't worry about the cost."

Joseph perked up at the news. "Then maybe we should order a bottle of champagne to celebrate."

"That sounds like a good idea," Brad concurred.

But as the meal progressed Brad wondered if this double-dating thing had been such a good idea after all. For one thing, his granddad had spent nearly twenty minutes expounding on the chances of the Cubs winning their division, until his grandmother had simply put her foot down and ordered, "No more baseball talk."

"What about football?" Joseph asked. "Basketball?"

Violet shook her head.

Joseph morosely sank into silence.

"It's a lovely view. I wish I'd brought along my little sketchbook," Violet said wistfully.

"It's just the ocean," Joseph retorted. "You can see it or Narragansett Bay from just about anyplace around here. After all, we do live on an island. Newport, Middletown and Portsmouth—they're all on Aquidneck Island. Not everyone realizes that."

"I've lived here as long as you have," Violet returned. "I know we're on an island! That doesn't mean I can't enjoy looking at the view!"

"We're also living in the smallest state in the nation," Joseph bragged to Sabrina.

She'd already known that, but could see that he was trying to impress her with his knowledge, so she smiled politely.

"Never play Trivial Pursuit with this man," Violet said in exasperation. "He knows every inconsequential fact there is to know."

Joseph beamed. "I even know the date shipbuilding started here in Newport. It was 1646!"

"Now, Joseph," Violet warned, "don't start on your history of shipbuilding."

"Why not? I'm sure Sabrina would be interested," Joseph insisted.

Violet sighed. "Maybe so, but Brad and I have already heard this speech fifty times before."

"Then don't listen," Joseph retorted. "Anyway..."

Brad could see the mistakes his grandfather was making by monopolizing the conversation, and he wanted to help him out. Besides, he *had* heard this speech at least fifty times. Maybe even a hundred! Brad didn't think he could handle hearing it again.

"Of course in those days Newport was a leading seaport," Joseph was saying. "Why, the town handled more cargo than New York. Or so I'm told. I wasn't there at the time, of course. After all, this was over three centuries ago."

Brad knew that by the time his grandfather had itemized the decade-by-decade occurrences in shipbuilding it would *feel* as if three centuries had crawled by!

"The next ship to go out in 1698, or was it 1696...?" Joseph paused.

It was the break Brad had been waiting for. "Yes, the ships in those days were certainly something, Granddad. Of course, some of the yachts we've got around today are pretty spectacular," Brad smoothly inserted. He then went on to share a few anecdotes about his escapades on some of the more luxurious yachts he'd either been on or worked on.

Sabrina was surprised to hear some of the places he'd visited—Fiji, the French Riviera. When he'd casually told her that he "worked his way around the world" she'd never imagined him in such jet-setting hot spots.

Then she heard him say, "But there was one beauty in particular that caught my fancy..." Brad sighed with the memory.

Sabrina gave him a suspicious look, wondering what the heck Brad was doing talking about past loves at a time like this.

Realizing Sabrina didn't know he was still talking about a yacht, Brad hurriedly went on. "It had a hydraulically operated table that disappeared into the floor. Talk about streamlined. Forget your gold-plated sinks and twenty-four karat gold faucets, I was more impressed by that table. Of course, a hundred-and-fifty-foot motor yacht large enough to carry a Bell Jet Ranger helicopter and a car is pretty impressive, too."

"What a life," Violet murmured.

"Your life hasn't been that bad," Joseph said defensively. "I might not have been able to buy you a big yacht, but I always made sure there was enough money for my family!"

Violet looked at him in surprise. "I never said you didn't."

"Money can't buy you happiness," Joseph stated.

Amen to that, Sabrina thought to herself. She wondered if Brad and his family realized how lucky they were to have each other. At least they cared enough *to* argue. It wasn't a lack of love that was the problem here, just a temporary lack of understanding.

Sabrina wished there was more she could do to make things right again. But she had a feeling this was one lesson Joseph was going to have to learn by himself.

"I never said money could buy happiness," Violet protested. "Happiness is something you have to find for yourself."

"Well, I know what makes Sabrina happy," Brad said as he gave her a wicked look.

Sabrina held her breath, afraid of what he might say. She wouldn't put it past him to announce that his kisses made her happy! So she tried heading him off before he revealed anything incriminating. "Needling me certainly makes *you* happy," she retorted.

"Is it needling you to say that turtle sundaes make you happy?" Brad countered innocently.

"Turtle sundaes? I like those myself," Violet admitted. "There's something about the combination of caramel and chocolate and pecans over vanilla ice cream that's just delicious."

"Mmm, delicious," Brad agreed, his eyes fixed on Sabrina's lips.

She couldn't believe he was flirting with her this way in front of his grandparents! She wanted to kick him under the table, but good manners prevented her from giving in to the temptation. So she had to make do with her best "behave yourself" look. It rolled off him like water off a duck's back.

"Let's make a toast," Brad said, topping off everyone's glass. They'd only finished half the bottle. "To the future and all the sweet things in life."

"Hear! Hear!" Joseph concurred.

As they all raised their glasses, Sabrina awaited Brad's next move. Sure enough, when their glasses touched, so too did their hands. The magical current was still very much alive between them. She nervously licked her lips—a mistake, because her movement only intensified the hunger in Brad's expressive eyes.

"Another toast," Joseph suggested heartily. "To Violet coming home tonight where she belongs."

The sharp clink of Violet's glass as she placed it on the table brought Sabrina's attention away from Brad and onto his grandmother.

"What's the matter?" Joseph asked.

"I think we've had enough champagne for one evening," Violet said.

"All right." Joseph set his glass on the table as well. "It's getting late, anyway. How are we supposed to get home, though? Brad drove me over in that little sports car of his. You and I won't both fit in it. Never mind, I'll just call a cab, I suppose."

"That won't be necessary," Violet stated. "We can go back the same way we came. Sabrina can drive me, and Brad can drive you."

"Or Sabrina could drive both of us to Middletown," Joseph suggested. "That would save Brad having to make the trip. Would you mind, Sabrina?"

"I mind," Violet declared. "I'm not going to Middletown."

"I thought we settled this already," Joseph said.

"You were mistaken," Violet retorted.

"Can't you see these two want to be alone?" Joseph said, pointing at Sabrina and Brad. "They don't need you getting in the way. It's time you stopped acting foolish and came on home with me. This nonsense has gone on long enough."

"If I'm in the way, I'll go stay at a hotel," Violet announced. "There are certainly enough of them in the area."

Seeing the hurt expression on his grandmother's face, Brad felt obliged to stick up for her. "You're not in the way. You can stay with me."

"It's not a problem for you?" Violet asked anxiously.

Brad shook his head.

"Well, it's a problem for *me*," Joseph declared. "Or doesn't anyone care about that? There's no reason for you not to come home tonight."

"Yes, there is," Violet replied. "This is exactly what I meant about not wanting to be taken for granted again. You just assumed that I would be going home with you."

"You're my wife. That's not such a strange assumption!"

"I think it would be best if we kept things as they are for the time being," Violet stated.

"What is it you want from me?" Joseph demanded in irritation.

"I want to be noticed. To be appreciated."

"Fine," Joseph shot back. "You're noticed. You're appreciated."

Sabrina could understand how Joseph's flippant tone of voice would only worsen Violet's anger. And that it did. "Don't patronize me!" Violet exclaimed furiously. "When you're ready to be serious, then give me a call. I might consider going out on another double date with you. Then again, I might not. Sabrina, would you mind driving me back to Brad's apartment now? I'm suddenly very tired."

"I'm tired, too," Joseph complained as Sabrina hurriedly escorted Violet from the premises. "What are you looking at me like that for?" Joseph demanded of Brad. "I thought you were on my side. Why didn't you tell her to come home with me?"

"It wouldn't have done any good. You heard her. She'd just have gone to a hotel."

"I don't know what she wants from me."

"It sounds like she wants a little old-fashioned courting, Granddad."

"Why would I want to court my own wife?" Joseph asked in bewilderment.

"Look at it this way," Brad said. "You'll be able to sweep her off her feet all over again."

"I'd like to toss her over my shoulder and drag her home right now," Joseph muttered.

"Not the best move, Granddad. She wants to be..." Brad paused, searching for the right word. "She wants to be *romanced*."

"I already romanced her once. When we were courting. That was enough."

"You were just a teenager then," Brad said. "Now you're a man of the world. Think how much better you could do now if you really put your mind to it."

"Seems like a lot of work," Joseph grumbled.

"Isn't she worth it?" Brad challenged.

"Yes, I suppose she is."

"There you go then."

"I wouldn't know how to date a woman these days. Besides you heard her, even if she did say yes, she wants you and Sabrina to come along. Who ever heard of double-dating with your own grandson?"

"It'll be a first for me, too," Brad wryly assured him. "But remember, we're Romanovskis. Are you going to tell me it can't be done?"

"Absolutely not! Say it can't be done, and we'll prove 'em wrong." Joseph picked up his still-full glass of champagne. "To catching the woman of our dreams."

"Amen to that," Brad agreed wholeheartedly.

"What makes men so stupid?" Violet demanded in exasperation.

Sabrina just shrugged, as she'd been doing for the past ten minutes while Violet indulged in a diatribe against the male of the species. She figured Violet wasn't really looking for an answer, she just needed to blow off some steam.

Besides, Sabrina didn't have any answers. Just more questions of her own. Like: what made her tremble when

Brad smiled at her in a certain way? Why couldn't she forget his kisses? When would she stop craving more of them?

The sound of the apartment door being unlocked distracted her from her brooding thoughts.

"Oh, good," Brad said as he entered the living room. "You're still here."

"Of course I'm still here," Violet replied. "You told me I could stay." Then, seeing the way Brad's eyes were focused on Sabrina, she said, "Oh. You meant you're glad Sabrina's still here. Yes, well, I'm just going to go on into the kitchen and make myself another pot of tea. I'm sure you two can amuse yourselves while I'm gone."

"Did you drive your grandfather home?" Sabrina asked, hoping to aim the conversation in a safe direction.

Brad nodded. "He wasn't too happy about it, however. He means well, you know."

"I'm sure he does. He just seems to be having a little trouble expressing himself."

"We made some headway tonight. At least they were talking to each other for a while there."

"I'm sure Violet will talk to Joseph if he calls her. Will he do that?"

"He's a Romanovski. We don't let our women get away from us without a fight."

Sabrina knew Brad wasn't just talking about his grandfather now. He was talking about himself as well. "Yes, well, it's getting late," she noted skittishly. "I'd better go."

"Thanks for driving her home for me. And for staying with her until I got here."

"No problem."

"Sabrina?"

"What?"

"Just this." He leaned down to kiss her. It was sudden and gentle, then fierce and hungry.

An entire week had passed since he'd kissed her down by the wharf. Sabrina told herself she should have gotten over him by now. Instead, her attraction to him kept on growing. She found herself responding to him, her lips softly but briefly clinging to his before she pulled away.

"What did you do that for?" she whispered.

"For my sanity." With a gentle finger, Brad traced her lips, which were still moist from his kiss. "I would have gone crazy if I hadn't kissed you again."

"I think you're already crazy," she said shakily. "Your grandmother is right in the other room. She could walk in here any second..."

As if on cue, Violet came into the living room. Seeing them together she said, "Oops. Am I interrupting something?"

"Of course not," Sabrina hurriedly denied, stepping farther away from Brad. "I was just on my way out." As in *out* of control, *out* of my mind, Sabrina silently completed. "Good night."

"Sleep tight," Brad added with a rakish smile.

Right.

The next morning Brad found his grandmother pulling the two remaining cans from a six-pack of beer he had in the fridge.

"It's a little early to be drinking, isn't it?" Brad asked in alarm.

"Silly boy." Violet put the cans back and held up the plastic rings that had held the cans together. "I'm just getting rid of this." She cut the plastic with a pair of scissors, methodically clipping and opening every ring. "Sabrina told me last night that these things are extremely dangerous to all kinds of wildlife, from squirrels to sea gulls. The poor things get stuck in these stupid rings and can end up getting strangled. I want to prevent that. You think you're getting rid of it when you throw something like this away, but it's really just ending up on some landfill somewhere or on a barge hauling garbage."

"Is that what you two were talking about when I walked in last night? Garbage?"

"And men," Violet added.

"Any reason for the combination?" Brad asked suspiciously.

"Should there be?"

"Now you're starting to sound like Sabrina. Is she telling you that you should strike out on your own?"

"Not at all," Violent denied. "*She'd* never tell me what to do, unlike everyone in my family. Would you believe that your father called me last night and had the nerve to lecture me about returning to your grandfather? Thank heavens your mother came on the line and told me he was full of prunes."

"Who was full of prunes? Granddad or Dad?"

"Both of them."

"Great." Brad thrust a hand through his already ruffled hair. "This really is turning into a battle of the sexes. Next thing I know, Mom will be moving in with me."

"She did mention something like that... There, there, no need to look so panicked," Violet reassured Brad with a grin. "I was only kidding."

"Thank heaven."

"Is my staying here with you a problem?" Violet asked in concern.

"No." He gave her a quick hug. "I told you yesterday that you're always welcome here."

"You're a good boy. And you've picked a good girl this time. I like Sabrina."

"You can just get that matchmaking look right out of your eyes," Brad told her.

"Why should I? Isn't that what you and Sabrina have been doing to me? Matchmaking? To get me and your grandfather back again. You think I haven't noticed? But I've also noticed what's going on between you and Sabrina." Violet nodded knowingly. "Definitely lots of chemistry there."

Brad almost choked on the orange juice he was drinking.

Violet solicitously patted him on the back. "What's the matter? Aren't I supposed to know about things like chemistry and sex appeal? Do you think I found your father and your two uncles under a cabbage someplace?"

"Of course not."

"I know more than you might think. I know you've got your grandfather's bedroom eyes and his stubborn nature. A powerful combination and hard for a woman to resist. Do you love Sabrina?"

Had Brad taken another sip of juice he would have choked on that one, too. But he'd wisely set the glass down the first time she'd caught him by surprise. "What is this?" he demanded in exasperation. "Why are you giving me the third degree?"

"Because you're my grandson and I love you."

"Then don't ask me questions I can't answer."

"Aha, so you *could* be in love with her. You're just not sure of your feelings yet."

"Stop twisting my words."

"Well, I think you'd be a fool to let her get away," Violet stated.

"Who says she's going anywhere? And who says I'd let her get away?"

"What are her feelings for you?"

"Maybe you should ask her," Brad replied without thinking. Seeing the gleam in his grandmother's eyes, he hastily retracted that statement. "On second thought, forget I ever said that. I don't want you mentioning anything to Sabrina."

"I can be very discreet," she assured him.

"I can do my own talking. If I want to ask her any questions, I'll ask her myself. Understood?"

"Yes."

"Besides you shouldn't be worrying about my love life at a time like this. You should be thinking about your own life and getting back together with Granddad."

"Have you ever noticed how much easier it is to work on other people's problems instead of your own?" Violet inquired philosophically.

Actually Brad had noticed that but he wasn't about to admit as much. "Will you accept if Granddad asks you out?"

"Providing he behaves himself."

"What does that mean?"

"It means that he asks me what *I'd* like to do for a change. And then agrees to spend the day doing what I want to do without complaining about it every second of the day."

"You're not talking about spending a day doing something like shopping, are you?" Brad countered cautiously.

"Of course not! I'm not expecting miracles from your grandfather. I know he hates to shop. No, I was thinking more along the lines of spending a Saturday afternoon on the beach. With you and Sabrina."

"Sounds reasonable enough."

"Have you taken Sabrina to the beach yet?"

"Not yet."

"Then it would be a nice opportunity for you, as well," Violet noted perceptively.

Brad knew all about opportunities and making the most of them. "I'll bet Granddad will be calling you *real* soon." Brad planned on making sure of it!

"Why eat on a beach?" Joseph demanded as he came to pick up Violet from Brad's apartment at the appointed time on Saturday afternoon. "All that sand gets in the food and makes it gritty. Much better to eat at home."

"Better for you, maybe," Violet retorted. "But it's a beautiful day—the sun is shining—and I think it would be nice to sit on the beach. Sabrina and Brad agreed with me, so stop being such an old fuddy-duddy."

"I am not old," Joseph protested.

"I don't think so, either," Violet agreed. "Which is why it irritates me when you start *acting* old."

"Come home with me," Joseph countered, "and I'll show you how young I am!"

"Not yet," Violet murmured. Brad watched in surprise as his grandmother fluttered her lashes like a pro. "Come to the beach and we'll see what happens."

Joseph made no further complaints as he ushered Violet out of the apartment. "We'll meet you there," Joseph told Brad, who still had to pick up Sabrina from her place.

"Fine."

"Don't be too long," Violet added, warning Brad not to try and pull a fast one by not showing up.

"We'll be there," he promised.

As he drove to Sabrina's place, Brad recalled the phone conversation they'd had the other night. "Are you going to insist on driving yourself to the beach or are you actually going to let me drive you?" he'd asked her.

"Your Corvette only seats two. Where is your grandmother going to sit?"

"In my grandfather's car. This is supposed to be a date, remember?"

"For them," she retorted. "Not for us."

That might have been what Sabrina thought, but Brad had other ideas. While he was glad that their joint matchmaking efforts appeared to be paying off, and that his grandparents were getting on better, he still chafed at not having the freedom to pursue Sabrina the way he wanted to. But it was difficult to chase her when his grandmother was keeping such close tabs on his movements.

No, first he had to get his grandparents settled and then he'd be free to devote all his attention to Sabrina. And the sooner, the better, as far as he was concerned.

SMOOTH SAILING

* * *

Brad had barely walked in the door of Sabrina's apartment when he was approached by a tomcat the size of a small dog.

"What do you feed this cat?" he asked in amazement.

"Whatever he wants," Sabrina replied.

"Wise decision. Best not to cross an animal the size of a lion cub."

Some might say it was best not to cross Brad, either, Sabrina noted. He looked lean and dangerously good-looking in a plain navy T-shirt and blue jeans.

"Where did you find this cat? The zoo?" Brad inquired.

"I didn't find Thomas, he found me when he was just a kitten and demanded that I bring him in from the cold."

"Smart cat," Brad murmured. "I'll have to try that trick sometime."

Now that Sabrina thought about it, Brad and Thomas did have certain things in common—they liked catching fish, they were both possessive, and they'd both walked into her life without an invitation. Brad was only in her life temporarily, however, she quickly reminded herself. But that was also how she'd ended up taking in Thomas—as a temporary measure that had become permanent.

"You and your cat are both staring at me very strangely," Brad noted. "Is your roommate an attack cat?"

"Thomas wouldn't hurt a fly," Sabrina maintained. She paused, having just recalled that Thomas loved to *eat* flies. "He wouldn't hurt most things," she revised.

Thomas arched his back and stretched, as if showing off his muscular strength. After all he was a male, so Sabrina excused the show-off display.

"Just sit down a minute," she told Brad. "I'm almost ready."

Brad sat on a wooden rocking chair that was surprisingly comfortable. Her place had a homey feel to it—he approved. He also approved of the way Sabrina looked. She had her long blond hair piled rather haphazardly, for her, on top of her head. She was wearing a pair of blue walking shorts and a white T-shirt that said Mother Nature Says Clean Up Your Room. Her feet, for the time being, were bare—leaving the long expanse of her legs exposed to his appreciative gaze.

"Nice. Very nice," he murmured. "But where's your swimsuit? Under the shorts?"

"I'm not wearing a swimsuit."

He raised an eyebrow. "You plan on skinny-dipping?"

"I'm not going in the water."

"Why not? I thought this would be the perfect time for me to give you a swimming lesson. My grandparents will be there to act as chaperons. Surely you don't think I'd try and drown you in front of them?"

"No, but..."

"Then go put on your suit," he told her. "You do have one, don't you?"

"Yes." She had one she used for sunning and hot-tubbing.

"Good. Go put it on."

"Forget it," she stated. Sabrina had deliberately chosen to wear shorts to the beach today because she didn't want Brad getting any ideas—about her, or about teaching her how to swim. She figured that he couldn't maneuver her into the water, or just plain toss her in, if she wasn't wearing a suit. Grandparents or no grandparents—where Brad was concerned, she'd discovered that it was better to be safe than sorry. "I already told you, I don't want a swimming lesson," she firmly reminded him.

He sighed. "We're back to that again, are we?"

"We're back to that. Why are you so set on teaching me to swim, anyway?" she demanded.

"Why are you so against the idea?" Brad countered.

"I asked you first," she pointed out.

Stalling for time, he repeated her question. "Why am I so set on teaching you how to swim? You mean aside from the obvious advantages of being able to hold you in my arms and have you completely at my mercy?"

"Yes," she agreed dryly. "Aside from those so-called advantages."

"Maybe I'm just trying to be helpful and do you a favor, ever think of that?"

"Nope."

He didn't know whether to be insulted or complimented. "You think I wouldn't do something without having an ulterior motive?"

"That's right."

"You think you know me pretty well, don't you?"

"I know that I'm not going to let you finagle me into taking swimming lessons from you, so you can just forget about it."

That was part of his problem, Brad acknowledged wryly. He couldn't forget anything about Sabrina. Not the way the sun lit her hair, or the floral scent of her perfume, or her classy walk. She was proving to be pretty damn memorable. Brad had yet to decide whether that was good or not.

Joseph was waiting impatiently for them at the beach's well-filled parking lot. "You didn't forget the food, did you?" he asked in concern.

"It's right here." Brad held up a picnic basket, which he'd bought at the deli along with the included luncheon fare of cold cuts, chilled jumbo shrimp, fresh bread, three kinds of salads and the best brownies this side of Hershey, PA.

"Good. I brought the blanket and I think I've already found us a spot. I staked it out and left your grandmother there to protect it," Joseph said.

"I think there's enough room for everyone," Brad replied dryly. "I don't think we really need to post a claim."

"On a weekday, maybe not. But it's a Saturday and we're not far off from Labor Day weekend—and you know what that means. With all the goings-on, not to mention the sailing regattas, the town will be packed to the rafters. So will the beach."

His grandfather was right. It was crowded, although not impossibly so. Besides, Brad told himself, that just meant that Sabrina didn't have as much space to scoot away from him when he got close to her. And he planned on getting plenty close to her.

He started out casually enough, with a jumbo shrimp. "You've got to try one of these," he told her. "They're great." Instead of handing over the appetizing piece of seafood to her, though, Brad retained possession of it and offered it to her—by holding it up to her lips.

Sabrina was not accustomed to being hand-fed, her only experience having been with the roast beef she offered her cat, Thomas. And then she'd been the feed*er*, not the feed*ee*.

When she hesitated, Brad wiggled the shrimp temptingly, reminding Sabrina of a fisherman wiggling his bait in an attempt to get a certain fish's attention. She warily reached out to cup her hand around his and bring the tasty-looking morsel a little closer to her mouth. This way she felt she had a little more control over the process.

That was her intention. The reality was that not only did she have the heady experience of his fingers brushing her lips, but also of the warmth of his hand beneath hers.

Did he realize the effect he had on her? Hopefully the sunglasses she wore to protect her eyes from the glare also protected her from his all-too-knowing gaze. And thankfully her hands were steady; the trembling was internal for the time being. But the effervescent excitement made her feel like a bottle of bubbly soda water that had been well and truly shaken up.

Was he still playing games with her? she wondered. Was he trying to teach *her* how to play games with *him*?

If so, she was a fast learner. She could tell that her touch affected him as well. So she allowed her fingers to curl confidingly around his hand as she delicately bit into the shrimp he held to her lips. With the second bite, she made sure to scrape her teeth ever so gently against the skin of his finger.

The fire in Brad's brown eyes told her he knew exactly what she was doing—knew and approved of it. He would try and make her pay for it later, of that she had no doubt, but for the time being she felt safe enough in the company of his grandparents.

So she allowed Brad to flirt with her and allowed herself to flirt back. But she drew the line at accepting Brad's offer to spread sunscreen over her exposed arms and legs. It was one thing to play with fire, another thing entirely to toss a lit match into gallons of gasoline!

Just the thought of Brad's tempting fingers smoothing the skin of her thighs was enough to make Sabrina reach for a cold drink.

"You look flushed," Violet noted in concern. "Are you sure you're not getting a sunburn? You have such fair skin you need to watch out."

Sabrina already knew she had to watch out, all right! Watch out for Brad. "I'm fine," she assured Violet.

"If you're warm you should try going down by the water," Violet suggested. "I know you don't swim, but it's nice just to get your feet wet."

"Sabrina is very hesitant about getting her feet wet," Brad stated. "She's the cautious type."

"The cautious type *is* the type that likes getting their feet wet," Sabrina retorted. "It's the gung-ho type that jumps in the deep end." To prove her point Sabrina got up and moseyed on down to the water.

She hadn't lied when she'd told Brad before that she wasn't afraid of the water. In fact, as a child she'd enjoyed spending time on this very beach. Of course her parents had been discussing the sorry state of the world's oceans at the time, so the outings had turned out to be educational rather than enjoyable ones. There had never seemed to be time to just sit back and enjoy the simple pleasures of sun, sand and surf. She'd almost forgotten how soothing the sound of the waves greeting the land could be, how powerfully rhythmic. Like the heartbeat of the planet.

Sabrina smiled. Her parents would probably approve of that bit of imagery.

"What are you smiling at?" Brad asked from her side. He was wearing a pair of black swimming trunks.

Sabrina couldn't answer his simple question for the life of her. All she could do was stand and stare at him. This was more of his male body than she'd ever seen unclothed before. His swimsuit wasn't racy by any means. It didn't have to be.

Brad didn't need to flaunt his masculinity, it was evident in every aspect of the man—from the way his mind worked to the set of his powerful shoulders, the rippling muscles of his golden-skinned chest and the slim tapering of his waist and hips.

The man even had great legs, she noted in exasperation. No bony knees on this guy. How was she supposed to keep fighting this attraction between them when he stood there looking so damned good?

A second later Sabrina gasped as an advancing wave splashed its way up to her knees. Engrossed as she'd been in Brad's appearance, she hadn't even seen it coming. The water, cool against her warm skin, jogged her back to reality.

"Nice going," Brad noted dryly. Standing beside her as he was, he'd gotten splashed, too. "Since I'm this wet, I may as well go on in."

She watched him run into the water and then dive under an incoming wave. Sabrina took two steps back, narrowly avoiding getting drenched yet again. Walking along the beach a ways, she soon fell into the habit of playing tag with the ocean, avoiding the wavelets as they tried to swirl up around her ankles. She resolutely refused to brood. The day was too beautiful to ruin it by worrying about her feelings for Brad. For once she'd give herself a break and turn off the inner voice that told her what was proper and practical. She'd let herself go—just for today.

When Brad came out of the ocean he was still streaming water. Standing next to her, he shook himself dry like a huge German shepherd. Drops of water flew in every direction, some of them hitting Sabrina, who quickly retreated. But Brad kept following her, showering droplets of water at her.

"Beast!" she declared amidst her laughter. His wolfish smile really was too endearing to resist.

As they joined Brad's grandparents, Sabrina was pleased to see them sitting close together, holding hands. Hesitant to interrupt them, Sabrina halted abruptly. Brad promptly plowed into her from behind.

"Hey, signal when you plan on making a stop," he told her, placing his hands on her waist to steady her.

Their actions attracted Joseph and Violet's attention. "There you two are," Violet said. "We wondered what happened to you. There are so many people here it's hard to see past everyone to the water front."

"Now that you two are back to watch the stuff, your grandmother and I are going to go for a little dip in the ocean," Joseph announced.

"We're definitely making progress," Brad announced once they'd left.

For a moment, Sabrina thought he was talking about making progress with her, before realizing he was referring to his grandparents. "It does look promising," she agreed.

"They were holding hands," Brad said. "I haven't seen them do that in ages."

Holding hands, Sabrina reflected dreamily. Now there was a lost art. Like top hats and curtsying, it too appeared to have fallen by the wayside in today's fast-paced, bottom-line world.

Brad ran a finger down her bare arm, one of his favorite ways of getting her attention. "What were you thinking about?"

"Lost arts," she murmured.

"Huh?"

"So much has changed in the lifetime of your grandparents. Think about it. When they were kids, automobiles were just being developed. Men wore hats, women wore gloves. Your grandparents survived the Depression and World War II. They even survived being interviewed by me."

"Hey, if they can survive having me as their grandson, they can survive anything. They're tough."

"And they're in love."

"Yeah. You ever been in love?" he neatly slipped in.

"I refuse to answer that question on the grounds that I might incriminate myself," she replied. Brad had no way of knowing that his question had hit a sore spot with her. Emotions were easy for him. The same wasn't true for her.

The loving looks passing between Joseph and Violet for the remainder of the day only served to remind Sabrina of her own limitations. She wondered at her ability to miss something she'd never had—that kind of intensely personal, emotional closeness with another human being. She probably wouldn't even know how to respond to it. Another gap in her education, she noted wryly.

They stayed until sunset, squeezing the last bit of enjoyment out of what had been, for Sabrina, a perfect day. The crowd soon thinned out, leaving only a few stragglers behind.

"We're going to head on home now," Joseph stated after a whispered consultation with Violet. "You two young folks can stay a while longer if you want."

Sabrina would have started gathering up her belongings had Brad not put his arm around her and stilled her movements.

"You go on ahead, Granddad," Brad said.

As Joseph took Violet by the hand and led her away, Sabrina overheard him asking his wife where she'd like to have dinner that evening.

Brad waved as they disappeared from view. Then hauling Sabrina into his arms, he planted an enthusiastic kiss on her mouth. "We did it!" he said triumphantly. "We got them back together again!" He kissed her again, longer this time. "We did it."

This time his husky words were whispered against her lips, allowing her to feel them as well as hear them. Then he stopped speaking altogether and concentrated all his attention on her. His kiss conveyed his feelings and his needs— only, Sabrina was too mixed up to sort them all out. She couldn't concentrate when he was doing such provocative things with his tongue.

As darkness fell so did Sabrina's defenses, leaving her prey to the prowling hunger throbbing within her. Her inhibitions were swept away by the passion, the need.

Before she knew what had happened, Sabrina found herself lying on the blanket with Brad pressed against her. It was heavenly having him so close to her. There wasn't one inch of her that wasn't in contact with him. She felt his every move. He was warm, so warm, and solid. She had an awesome craving to touch him.

With eager fingers she undid the shirt he'd only recently buttoned against the cool, evening air. There was no coolness any longer. Only fiery heat. Radiating from his body to hers, from her mouth to his. She could feel the throbbing of his heart beneath her palm as she stroked the rippling smoothness of his bare chest. And she could feel the strength of his arousal as he shifted against her.

Like silent thieves, his hands stole beneath her T-shirt, robbing her of breath and sanity as he deftly released the front fastening of her bra. Now there was nothing to prevent him from plundering the riches he found there, the smooth lushness of her breasts fitting into the welcoming cup of his palms.

Sabrina murmured her wholehearted approval of his actions, arching against him. What little rationality she had remaining was stolen away by the magical persuasion of his thumb brushing over one rosy peak.

Their clothing provided a sheltering cover for their clandestine activities, adding an element of mystery to the building excitement. The learning was done purely by touch and taste. Discoveries were made and pleasures celebrated.

Groaning his delight, Brad rolled with her until they rested on their sides. By now, Sabrina's hair had come undone and he eagerly combed his fingers through the silky strands, tunneling his hand beneath the golden mass in a lifting and smoothing motion that was surprisingly arousing. His other hand continued to drive her wild as he lingered over his explorations beneath her T-shirt—each caress inspiring yet another surging thrill of desire.

When she slid her leg between his, Sabrina was rewarded for her boldness by a kiss so sensually intimate that she felt as if she were vibrating with need. She could actually feel the hunger humming within her, and within him.

The beat was the same, primitive, erotic, darkly enticing—beckoning her closer and closer to the point of no return.

Eight

Things were getting out of hand, Sabrina realized hazily, and they were getting that way *fast*. They had to stop. *Now!* She pulled away abruptly. Tempting as their passion was, its volatile intensity had also been somewhat frightening.

Brad didn't fight her decision. It was as if he, too, recognized how close they'd come to falling over the edge of an emotional volcano and into the scalding lava. Besides, they *were* still on a public beach.

Sitting up, Sabrina tightly wrapped her arms around her bent knees, as if by doing so she could forcibly hold back the tides of desire still churning within her.

"Yikes!" Sabrina didn't realize she'd actually murmured the word aloud until Brad chuckled huskily.

"Ditto," he agreed, his voice soft and rough.

"That was close."

"Not close enough." He trailed his finger down her bare arm. "Come back to my place."

"Your grandmother might still be there," she reminded him.

"I have a feeling she's home in her own bed tonight," Brad said, caressing the ultrasensitive skin of Sabrina's inner arm.

"This is happening too fast." Sabrina scooted away before he could tempt her further. "I only met you again two weeks ago...."

"Two and a half weeks ago," he corrected her.

"That's not enough time. I'm not the type of woman who goes to bed with a man just because I might be physically attracted to him."

"Ah—" Brad pounced on her comment "—then you do admit that you are attracted to me?"

Sabrina sighed restlessly. "It wouldn't do me much good to deny it, would it? Not after what we just shared. But that doesn't mean I'm ready to act on that need yet."

"Why not?"

"Because I'm not like that. You said yourself that I'm the cautious type."

"Great. You're the cautious type and I'm not known for my patience."

"It's just one of many differences between us."

"I'm more interested in our similarities," Brad murmured, brushing her long hair aside so that he could lightly kiss the nape of her neck. "In the things we share. And we shared a hell of lot just now. We should be sharing even more."

"No, we shouldn't. Not here. Not now."

"You're right," he agreed. "Not here, not now." His lips brushed her ear as he huskily whispered, "At my place, in about five minutes."

It wasn't easy but she maintained her resolve. "Dreamer."

"All right, so it takes *ten* minutes to get to my place."

"More like fifteen, but that's not what I meant."

"I know what you meant," he said. "Doesn't mean I have to like it."

"Are you going to be difficult?" she asked ruefully.

"Who me? Of course not. I'm an astute kind of guy, remember?" He reluctantly released her.

Leaning over, she softly kissed his cheek. "Thanks."

"Don't mention it. And I mean *don't* mention it. We stay here talking any longer and what few good intentions I have are going to go right out the window," he warned her curtly.

What's wrong with you? Brad asked himself as they walked back to his car moments later. You could have had her back there. You could have convinced her to come home with you.

But she wouldn't have stayed. No one makes me do anything, she'd told him once before. He'd wanted to prove her wrong. Instead he'd proved that she had an incredible hold on him. Why else would he have let her go?

And why else would that little kiss she'd placed on his cheek a few minutes ago have had such a powerful effect on him? It was more than just chemistry or sexual attraction. This was different, something he hadn't experienced before. Liking, maybe? In addition to lust? Did that equal love? This certainly felt closer to it than he'd ever been before.

It was a disconcerting proposition. Brad wasn't really eager to make a fool of himself over her again, the way he had as a teenager—that's why he'd needed to feel in control. But now he was beginning to suspect that he hadn't *really* been in control since she'd first walked into his office and flashed her big blue eyes at him. He had a desire for Sabrina that just wouldn't quit. Desire or love? Or both? he wondered.

During the drive back to her apartment Sabrina's thoughts remained on Brad. The faint light from the dashboard highlighted the angular lines of his face. And his lips.

She definitely had a thing for those lips of his. She was fascinated by them—by the taste and the feel of them.

Only now did she admit that she'd been silently eyeing his mouth ever since he'd tempted her with that shrimp earlier that afternoon. She'd imagined him kissing her, but those imaginings couldn't hold a candle to the real thing. She should have been worrying about what could have happened, what *almost* had happened, but all she could think about was how incredibly sexy his kisses were.

Dreamily closing her eyes, Sabrina replayed those intimate moments in her mind. When she felt his fingers brushing her cheek, she thought it was part of her fantasy. As she reached up to hold the memory of his touch against her skin, her hand collided with his.

Her eyes flew open. Shocked, Sabrina finally realized that the car had stopped and that they'd reached her apartment building.

"You were smiling," Brad noted softly. "What were you thinking about?"

Feeling foolish at getting caught daydreaming, Sabrina said, "It's getting late. I'd better go."

His hand on her shoulder stopped her. "Just one kiss," he huskily coaxed her. "I'll keep my hands to myself, I promise."

Brad was as good as his word, but it made no difference. The second his lips brushed hers, the fires flared again and raged until they were almost out of control. Tongue to tongue, heartbeat to heartbeat. It was over all too soon, but Sabrina knew that her resistance was already at a dangerously low level.

Fumbling with her seat belt, she jumped out of his car and rushed into her apartment building. If she'd stayed with him a second longer she'd have melted at his feet and done whatever he wanted.

But she wasn't ready for that yet—she had to wait until her emotional needs caught up with her physical ones.

Sabrina worried that that day might never come, however. It was entirely possible that a physical attraction to Brad might be the only thing she was capable of feeling. She wasn't frigid by any means, but the ability to emotionally commit to someone had proved to be damned elusive for her.

She'd eventually come to believe that she just didn't have the emotional wherewithal to love someone—to provide them with those special feelings of support and warmth. Since she'd grown up without feeling loved herself, she was afraid she lacked experience in that particular emotional department.

And what about Brad's emotions? a little voice in her head taunted her. It hadn't been that long ago that he'd resented and disliked her. Why should she trust him now? Could his feelings for her really have changed that drastically? Or were his recent attempts to seduce her just a smoke screen for his true intentions? Did he have some kind of plan up his sleeve? Sabrina sighed. So many questions. So few answers.

The sound of the phone ringing jangled her thoughts. It was Brad calling her from his car phone.

"Stop brooding," he told her, as if he'd been able to gauge her mood over the phone line. "And don't for one minute think you can climb back up into that ivory tower of yours. We're going to see each other again. We're going to kiss and drive each other crazy with need. And then we're going to make love. It's going to happen. For my sanity's sake I hope it's sooner rather than later, but it *is* going to happen."

The certainty in his voice threw her. "Don't corner me, Brad."

"If I'd cornered you," he growled, "you'd still be at the beach and we wouldn't both be sitting here with a powerful itch that hasn't been scratched."

"Is that what I am to you?" she demanded. "An itch?"

"You're the woman who's driving me crazy. You're the one I haven't been able to get out of my mind since I was seventeen. You're the one—period. So don't think you can run away from me."

She was surprisingly touched by his words. They weren't particularly romantic, but they were pure Brad—direct and to the point. For the moment his bluntness reassured her doubts. "I wasn't planning on running," she said softly.

"You weren't?" He sounded nonplussed by her admission.

"Like I told you on the beach, I admit that I want you...."

"I'll be right in!" he muttered.

"But I'm not ready yet," she hurriedly finished. "I need more time."

"Which means what?"

"Just what I said. I need more time. Is that so much to ask?"

"Feeling the way I am right now, it is. But I'm a Romanovski. I don't give up easily."

"You don't give up at all," Sabrina returned.

"Right. Remember that."

"I'm telling you, Thomas, he's not going to give up," Sabrina told her solidly built tomcat. She had to talk to someone and, since it was three in the morning, Thomas was the only one around and awake. He'd been practicing for the Indy 500 down her hallway, a favorite pastime of his, and once he'd heard her moving around in bed, he figured it was time to involve her in the game. So he'd come charging into the bedroom and leapt onto the bed with his toy mouse in his mouth. Since she was awake she might as well be playing with him.

Sabrina absently tossed the toy across the room. Thomas was after it in a flash.

"What did you think of him?"

The cat dumped the mouse in her lap.

"Did you like him?"

Thomas kept his eyes on the mouse, refusing to be distracted by her questions. She tossed it for him. He was back with it a moment later. "Are all cats this persistent or is it just you? Brad's persistent, too. I'm just not sure why. Since I practically melted in his arms, I don't know if I still qualify for being a challenge. Of course, there is the matter of our past, such as it was. He said I'd been on his mind since he was seventeen, but I'm not sure if that was a compliment or not. What do you think, Thomas?"

The cat yawned and settled down—on her foot—to wash himself.

"You're a big help," she grumbled. "Can't you at least give me a sign? Purr if you like Brad, growl if you don't trust him."

Thomas just closed his eyes and went to sleep. So did Sabrina... several hours later.

During the next two weeks, Brad gave Sabrina the time she'd requested, which was just as well since she was inundated at work. That didn't mean that he didn't make his presence felt, however. On those evenings when she was tied up at work, he'd send over a hot pizza with her name spelled out on it in black olives.

When she was working, the hours went by very quickly, since this was one of the busiest times of the year for them at Memories. Guy had been doing more than his fair share of being obnoxious, but she'd been able to handle him so far. She couldn't wait to finish that job so she could get rid of him once and for all.

As for Brad, he remained in her thoughts, regardless of what she was doing. He called her twice a day. And when they did meet, the old black magic continued working its powerful spell on her.

Today Brad had hijacked her from work, announcing he was taking her to some as yet undisclosed location. She hadn't protested too loudly, since she was sick of being cooped up in the editing room anyway. Besides, since she'd worked on weddings the past two weekends, this was the first Saturday afternoon she'd had off and what had she done to celebrate that fact? Gone in to catch up on some editing she had to do. Brad had said he simply couldn't allow such a thing to happen—he had to save her from herself and the massive broadcast-quality tape deck she'd been hunched over.

"The fresh air will do you good," he told her as they drove out on Purgatory Road. "It's starting to feel like fall, already. Can you tell?"

Sabrina could tell that she was staring at Brad's mouth again. "Um, yes," she agreed absently.

He shot her a sidelong glance. "I like your hair that way."

"What way?" Her hair was loose, she hadn't had time to do much with it.

"Blowing in the wind. It makes you look more touchable."

"It gets in the way."

"You're not planning on cutting it, are you?" he asked in alarm.

"There are days when I'm tempted, but I guess I'm too cautious to have it all chopped off."

"This is one case where I agree with you being cautious."

"You don't think I should cut my hair?" she asked as he pulled the Corvette into the parking lot for Second Beach.

Brad shook his head. "Never."

Recognizing their location, she said, "Why are we at the beach? I hope this isn't another attempt to teach me how to swim," she cautioned him.

"You do more than just swim on a beach, you know."

"I know," she murmured, remembering the heated embraces they'd shared. Although they hadn't gotten that out of control again, it was only because Sabrina was determined to keep her wits about her. It hadn't been easy.

"Come on. I want to show you something. Here—" he handed her the navy double-breasted blazer she'd brought along "—be sure to put this on. It's cooler by the water."

"What about you?" she asked, indicating his brown shirt and jeans. His shirt might be long-sleeved, but he had those sleeves rolled up clear to his elbows.

"I'm warm-blooded," Brad replied.

"I had noticed that," she said wryly.

"Did you now? That's encouraging." He put his arm around her shoulder and brought her close to his side. "Let's go."

"You still haven't told me exactly where it is we're going."

"To my special place." He glanced down at her and frowned. "Don't you ever wear jeans?"

"Not to the office," she retorted. "Besides, I didn't realize I was going to be kidnapped by a pirate today, so I wasn't able to dress for the occasion." Personally she thought her navy slacks and navy-and-white striped top were rather nice—classy yet casual.

"At least you're wearing sensible shoes."

"Now you make me sound like a schoolmarm," she grumbled.

He kissed her in a way that said he didn't find her the least bit schoolmarmish. He kissed her as if she were the most desirable woman in the world. She liked it. Too much.

By the time Brad reluctantly lifted his lips from hers, Sabrina's heart was pounding like a wild thing.

"You'll do," he noted huskily. "Come on—" he took her by the hand "—let's go."

Sabrina was already clambering over the rocks at the end of the beach before her mind cleared. They were heading away from the sand dunes and toward Sachuest Point.

"Is there any particular reason why we're out here today?" Sabrina asked breathlessly.

"I thought we should talk."

"We can't talk somewhere that's a little more easily accessible?"

"I would have thought that trekking would be right up your alley, what with your environmental parents and all." Brad noticed the way Sabrina stiffened when he mentioned her parents. This wasn't the first time it had happened. "Relax, I'm not going to verbally attack your precious parents."

"I should hope not. You've never even met them."

"And you never talk about them."

"That's not true. I talked about them that day at your grandparents' house."

"That was weeks ago."

"My family isn't as close as yours is, okay?" she said defensively.

"Okay. But I get the feeling there's something else."

She pulled away. "If this is just going to be an interrogation..."

He tugged her back to him. "It's not an interrogation. I'm curious about you, that's all."

"Why?"

"Because you're the best damn kisser I've ever known and you're the sexiest lady I've ever met," he promptly returned.

Sabrina couldn't help herself. She cracked up. "You've got such a way with words, Brad."

"I call 'em as I see 'em."

"How much farther is it to this special place of yours?"

"We're almost there," he assured her.

Given the fact that they were surrounded by a veritable rock dump, Sabrina wasn't sure how he could tell one boulder from another—but he headed straight for one in particular, from which he promised a wonderful view. Yet again, Brad was true to his word. Sachuest Point jutted out into the water with uncompromising stubbornness, providing them with a front-row seat to some absolutely spectacular coastal scenery.

Waves crashed against the shore while the sun glittered on the water, creating millions of shimmery diamonds on its blue surface. Squinting her eyes against the glare, Sabrina noticed a trim sailboat skimming its way across the horizon, sails billowing in the wind. At that moment she could understand Brad's love for both the sea and the ships that cleaved its waters. There was a salty magic here—a fantasy of speed and endurance, rhythm and eternity. Looking up, she saw sea gulls riding the air currents the same way the sailboat rode the water currents, both equally graceful in their flight.

"Being out here always makes me feel better," Brad murmured. "Helps me put things in perspective when I've had a bad day."

Sabrina's attention immediately shifted from the scenery to the man sitting so close beside her. "Did you have a bad day today?"

"I've had a string of them. Yesterday one of my workers broke his arm, which makes me shorthanded. No pun intended."

Sabrina only now realized that she still knew very little about his work. "Does that mean you'll have to do more of the installation work yourself?"

Brad nodded. "I do a fair amount of it already, especially the more complicated systems. But my work crew does most of the basic installation. Several boat manufacturers subcontract us to do that kind of work for them. I'm going to have to find more help in a hurry, or miss some important deadlines."

Even though he was the one who'd kidnapped her, Sabrina felt a twinge of guilt that he was here with her when he had so much to do. "Maybe we should head back so you can get some work done."

Brad shook his head at her suggestion. "I need a break. So do you. We've hardly seen each other at all this week."

"It's been wild at Memories, too."

"At least most of the summer crowds have gone home and traffic has returned to a more bearable level."

"I used to be a member of those summer crowds."

"Don't remind me. I don't want to talk about the past."

She wondered why that was. Could it be that Brad still harbored some resentment toward her because of the past? After all, he *had* accused her of being a spoiled rotten and selfish teenager. Did that feeling linger on? Is that why he avoided talking about those days?

"Then what do you want to talk about?" she asked. A slight edge of aloofness had crept into her voice, but she couldn't help it. Brad's avoidance of the past bothered her.

"I want to talk about us."

Sabrina looked at him with wary expectancy. "Yes? What about us?"

"You said you wanted time, and I've given you time, right?"

"You've given me two weeks."

"Which is twice as long as we'd known each other before," Brad pointed out.

"Is this your way of saying your patience is up?" she inquired.

"Let's just say it's wearing a little thin around the edges. I want to know where I stand with you," he said bluntly.

"And are you willing to tell me where *I* stand with *you*?" she returned with equal candor.

"You already know where you stand."

"Now you're doing what your grandfather did, assuming other people already know things so you don't have to say them."

"What do you want me to say?"

"Whatever you want to say. Maybe you should start with telling me why I've been on your mind since you were seventeen," she suggested in a determined tone of voice. "You never did explain that comment. I suspect it's more because you wanted to throttle me than because you wanted to kiss me."

"I already said I don't want to talk about the past," Brad said.

"It made us what we are today. And in our case, it's particularly relevant," she maintained.

"All right. You've been on my mind because..."

"Yes?" Sabrina prompted.

This conversation was not going the way Brad had thought it would. He wasn't supposed to be the one making confessions here—*she* was. "Because I couldn't forget you," he admitted impatiently, as if that much should have been obvious. "You made a big impression on me."

"Not a favorable one, though. You've told me so yourself. You thought I was some rich spoiled kid."

"You were also gorgeous," he said.

Sabrina laughed, certain he must be teasing her. "I most certainly was not! My legs were too long and I was too tall for my age."

"Trust me. You were gorgeous. You still are."

"Then tell me this—why were you so hostile toward me? Even when I came into your office, you were still... I don't know... simmering with anger or something."

He shifted uneasily. "You were imagining things."

"No, I wasn't. Brad, come on. Tell me the truth. I think I deserve that much, don't you? How can we move forward if there's this anchor keeping us chained to the past?"

Brad didn't know what to say, where to start. His thoughts were in a jumble and he had to get this right. "Look, I'll admit that when my sister first told me that you were coming to my office, I considered the possibility of getting even." He'd done more than just *consider* it, but didn't think he needed to go into details.

Sabrina frowned. "Getting even for what? What did I ever do to you?"

"That's just it," he retorted in exasperation. "You never did anything to me. You ignored me every damn summer. You looked right through me as if I wasn't even there!"

"That's because you were always making fun of me."

"I was eating my heart out for you," he ground out. It wasn't an easy admission for him to make.

"What are you talking about?"

Great. Now she had to go and play dumb. Brad glared at her, but she was staring at him with genuine disbelief. "You know what I'm talking about," he said.

"I certainly don't. You had a girlfriend with you, a different one each year, but always a dark-haired beauty—" she wanted to say floozy, but restrained herself "—with a skimpy halter top."

"Because I couldn't have you! You were this classy, stuck-up blond angel who wouldn't even give me the time of day. I thought you were like all the other stuck-up jerks you hung around with."

"I thought you hated me. I thought you had a thing against rich girls, or rich blond girls."

"I had a thing, all right. *For* one rich blond girl, not *against* her."

"Well, how was I supposed to know that?" she retorted. "You may be able to read minds, but I sure couldn't. I still can't. Are you telling me that your interest in me has been caused by a need for revenge?" Her voice reflected her pain.

"The need is for you," he quietly assured her, "not for revenge. I thought I knew you, but now I realize that I never knew you at all. I had a preconceived idea about you that wasn't right. Can you understand that?"

Sabrina nodded slowly. Yes, she could understand that, because she'd felt the same way about him. She'd thought she'd known who Brad Romanovski was, only to find that she'd never really known him at all.

"I had a preconceived idea about you, too," she admitted. "I thought you were a troublemaker out to make my life difficult. I had no idea you were the least bit interested in me. I really thought you hated me. And as for my being stuck-up, I was always nervous when I came here for the summer. I had to get to know everyone all over again. I didn't want them to know that I felt nervous, so I tried to act super calm and in control. Whenever you were around you made me feel even *more* nervous, so naturally I acted even more distant."

"I didn't think girls like you got nervous," Brad noted dryly.

"Now you know better. And you were right when you said that I didn't have very good judgment in my selection of friends. Since I've come back to town I've realized that I have nothing in common with those people—especially now." She paused before making her decision. The time had come to come clean with him. "There's something you don't know about me, something Eliot said I should have told you about in the beginning."

Brad's heart stopped. This sounded ominous. Was she married?

After taking a deep breath, Sabrina stated, "I'm not rich. My parents were wealthy, yes. But eight years ago, right after I graduated from college, they donated all their money to assist a worldwide environmental organization. They spend all their time working for that organization, basically for room and board. No celebrity tennis tournaments," she said, reminding him of a comment he'd made when she'd first mentioned her parents' interest in the environment. "They don't even own a tennis racket. They're involved with field trips to the Amazon, that sort of thing."

The first thing Brad felt was relief that her confession was such an irrelevant one. It did fill in some missing gaps, though. "I wondered why you were living in that apartment of yours," he murmured.

"There's nothing wrong with my apartment," she said defensively.

"No, I didn't mean it that way. I like it. It's just that it's not..."

"In the ritziest part of town," she completed. "I know that. I have a budget I have to keep to these days. No more long leisurely trips to Europe or shopping sprees at Saks Fifth Avenue. It's strictly local three-day weekend jaunts and outlet store sales for me these days."

"Why didn't you tell me this sooner?" Brad demanded.

"Because I thought you'd accuse me of putting on some poor-little-rich-girl routine, say that I was trying to get your sympathy or something. You have to admit, you weren't very nice the one time I did mention my family. Besides, I was getting sick of all the strange looks I've been getting as people find out what my parents did."

"What kind of strange looks?"

"As if they're wondering if insanity runs in the family."

"I don't think there's anything insane about putting your money where your mouth is," he stated.

"You don't?"

"Of course not. And speaking of mouths, I know where I want mine to be..." He nuzzled the skin behind her ear.

"I thought you wanted to talk."

"We've talked enough. Now it's time for action."

But there was only so much action they could accomplish on a boulder that tilted at almost a forty-five degree angle. Brad made the best of the situation, however. Lowering Sabrina to a semireclining position, he threaded his fingers through her hair and kissed her, gently nibbling at the softness of her skin as if she were a luscious delicacy laid out on a platter for his enjoyment.

And enjoy her, he did. He savored the sweet taste of her lips, the silky softness of her long hair, the yielding warmth of the body beneath his. He still couldn't get over the immediate combustion between them. Sabrina had the ability to arouse him with just one look. Her kisses set him on fire while her soft moans of pleasure almost made him lose his self-control.

Sabrina found herself between the proverbial rock and a hard place—between a boulder and the throbbing firmness of Brad's arousal, between wanting to go all the way and knowing they had to stop. But not yet, she told herself as she basked in the sensual glow of his embrace.

It felt so good, so darkly tempting to be kissing him and to lose herself in the intimacies of every tantalizing thrust of his tongue. She responded with a similarly forceful hunger of her own as his lips sought hers again and again.

This time it was Brad who drew away, albeit with extreme reluctance.

"Your time's almost up," he warned her unsteadily, "because I can't take much more of this."

Sabrina knew he was right. She couldn't take much more, either. She had to reach a decision soon—very soon.

Al was waiting for Brad upon his return to the office. Brad had forgotten all about agreeing to meet his friend for a beer that evening.

"Where have you been, buddy?" Al demanded as he straightened from his position propping up the doorway to the building. "You're late."

"Sorry about that. I was out at Sachuest Point."

"Fishing?"

"I was with Sabrina," Brad replied.

"You took her out there to your secret fishing place? You sly old dog, you. And did you tell her you'd never taken another woman there before?"

"I never *have* taken another woman there before."

Al slapped Brad on the back with a force that would have made a lesser man wince. "Brilliant move on your part."

"I'm not making moves. This isn't a game to me. Not anymore."

"Oh-oh. I don't like the sound of that one bit," Al said.

"I wasn't too happy about it myself at first," Brad wryly admitted. "But I really care about her, Al."

"I knew it! You're caught—hook, line and sinker."

"Yeah, I guess I am," Brad noted dazedly. "And you know what? I shouldn't be standing here talking to you about it. I should be talking to the sexy lady who's caught me. Thanks, buddy."

"Thanks for what?" Al asked in confusion. "Hey, where are you going?" he called after Brad.

"To find Sabrina."

Sabrina knew she'd promised Brad she'd head straight home, but she really did have to finish this editing job. She only had about another hour's worth of work to do and then she'd be home free.

The sound of someone pounding on the company's front door startled her. It was probably Brad, checking up on her. No one else knew she was there. As she unlocked the door her thoughts were on what she'd say to Brad, if he let her say anything at all before kissing her.

"Brad, I—"

Too late she realized her mistake. It wasn't Brad, but Guy Smythe-Jones. And he'd definitely had a few too many, judging by his unsteady demeanor and the unmistakable odor of whiskey about him. Now she knew who the malevolent steely-eyed look of Brad's stuffed fish had reminded her of—Guy. The alcohol he'd consumed had dulled the steely gaze somewhat, but the malevolence was still there. She had to get rid of him and fast.

"We're closed, Guy," she firmly and coolly stated. "You'll have to come back during regular business hours."

"Don' wan' regular business," Guy slurred. "Wan' you."

By the time Sabrina realized what Guy had in mind it was too late to avoid him as he made a surprisingly speedy grab for her.

"You're drunk," she said in disgust, any pretense of client courtesy flying out the window. Her job description did not include putting up with this kind of behavior. "Let me go this instant or you'll be singing soprano in the boys' choir!"

Guy laughed uproariously. "I always knew you weren't a real lady."

"I mean it, Guy. Let me go!"

"Whatsa matter? Don' you like me?"

"No. Especially not when you're drunk."

"You never liked me sober, either," he accused her.

She tried to reason with him. "When Eliot hears about this he'll cancel our contract with you and you'll never get your renovations documented on video tape."

"Don' care. I'll just hire someone else," he said arrogantly. "I'd rather have you than some stupid video tape anyway."

When he pulled her closer, Sabrina positioned herself to make her next move, recalling those self-defense lessons she'd taken in Boston. "I'm telling you for the last time, Guy. Let me go."

"What'll you do if I don't? Make me sing soprano?"

"If I have to," Sabrina replied.

The calm certainty of her voice made Guy pause. She felt his arms loosen their hold on her, but before he released her completely, the door suddenly opened.

"Sabrina, I thought you were going home..." Brad's voice trailed off as he took in the scene before him—Sabrina standing there pushing at Guy, who had his grubby hands on her. "What the hell is going on here?" Brad growled.

Then, without waiting for an answer because he could *see* what was going on, Brad launched himself at Guy. Grabbing the drunken man, Brad yanked him away from Sabrina and decked him with one mighty punch.

Nine

Brad looked down at the jerk who had been a thorn in his side since he'd been fifteen. This wasn't the first time Brad had flattened Guy Smythe-Jones—or Guy *Smut*-Jones, as he preferred to call him. But it was the first time he had done so as an adult. He thought he'd outgrown the need to settle things with his fists, but the second Brad had seen the piece of scum manhandling Sabrina, he'd seen red.

"You'll be sorry for this," Guy was mumbling. "I'll make sure you never do business in this town again, Romanovski."

Brad was not impressed by Guy's threats. "I'm giving you until the count of three to get out of here," he growled as Guy stumbled to his feet. "One, two..."

"You'll be sorry," Guy repeated before leaving.

"Brad, you shouldn't have done that," Sabrina said once they were alone.

Brad turned to her in astonishment. "What the hell are you talking about? You expect me to stand by doing nothing while that piece of horse manure paws you?"

"I had the situation under control. I was about to take care of it myself."

"Didn't look that way to me."

"You burst in here so fast that I don't see how you could have taken the time to look or survey the situation," she returned.

"Let me get this straight." The stormy softness of his voice indicated that his patience, such as it was, was quickly running out. "You're angry with me because I came to your defense?"

"No, I'm angry with you because you've let your anger make a bad situation even worse. You heard what Guy said. He's going to make trouble for you."

"He can try. But he won't get anywhere. His reputation is already on the skids, and it won't be helped any when the news gets around that I caught him manhandling my woman."

Brad's words infuriated her. *His* woman? "So this is a territorial battle between you two men, is that it? I just happen to be the territory in question, but otherwise this is none of my concern, right?"

"I never said that."

"You implied it."

"Look, the bad blood between me and that idiot goes way back. This isn't the first time I've knocked his lights out."

"Oh, that makes me feel much better," she noted sarcastically. "So the fight actually had nothing to do with me at all now. It was just an old grudge match between you two guys. That's just great!"

"It wasn't a fight. He didn't even throw one measly punch."

"Excuse me for not being precise on ringside terminology," she shot back.

"That's okay."

"No, it's not okay! You shouldn't have hit him. Guy has a lot of influence in this town and he can make trouble for you."

"I can look out for myself."

"So can I."

"Right," Brad snorted in disbelief. "What were you planning on doing to the jerk? And what was he doing in here in the first place? What were *you* doing here, for that matter?" He angrily fired one question after another at her. "You told me you were going home."

"I had some work to finish first. When Guy came to the door, I thought it was you checking up on me," Sabrina said.

Her answer only further inflamed Brad's temper. "You mean you let him in without even knowing who it was? Of all the idiotic..." Words temporarily failed him. "Do you know how stupid that is?" he shouted. "How dangerous? What if I hadn't seen the lights on in here when I drove by? What if I'd gone on to your apartment instead? Do you have any idea what could have happened if I hadn't come along when I did?"

"Well, for one thing, we wouldn't have him running around town trying to ruin your business," she pointed out, offended by Brad calling her idiotic and stupid.

Brad's expression was thunderous. "I can't believe you're taking his side in this!"

"I'm not taking his side. I'm just saying that you can't use your fists to settle every disagreement. We're adults now, Brad. I've been able to handle Guy in the past..."

"Wait a minute," he interrupted her. "You mean this wasn't the first time he's given you trouble?"

"It's the first time he's been so aggressive, but he's made a nuisance of himself before and I've been able to handle the situation."

"Why didn't you tell me about it?"

"Probably because I was afraid you'd have a fight with him, which is exactly what happened."

"You should have told me immediately. I can't believe that you've been letting him get away—"

"He hasn't gotten away with anything," she hotly denied.

"It looked like he was getting away with plenty when I walked in here."

"So now it's my fault. I suppose you think I egged him on or something?"

"Did you?" he shot back.

"I'm not even going to dignify that question with an answer," she retorted coldly. "I think you'd better leave."

He glared at her. "And I think you'd better realize that I'm not one of your ritzy well-mannered friends who turn the other cheek when their woman is being manhandled. If you're looking for that kind of lapdog, Golden Girl, you're looking at the wrong man." Brad turned on his heel and walked out.

Sabrina held on to her composure until she got home. Then the tears came with a vengeance. How could Brad have accused her of leading Guy on? Was violence his answer to every problem? Didn't he know that she only wanted what was best for him? But no, he was too concerned with his macho grudge against Guy to pay any attention to how she felt about anything.

It was as if Brad considered her to be some kind of trophy—just like that damn fish he had on his wall! Was that all she meant to him? A challenge to catch so that he could display her as proof of his male prowess?

She shouldn't be crying, Sabrina told herself as she wiped the tears away. She should be angry. Furious. And she was. But she was also hurt. And when she was hurt, she withdrew to avoid further pain. She was like a turtle that way.

Brad, however, was like nitroglycerin—volatile and quick to explode. She could definitely vouch for that, because she'd just had the misfortune of standing too close during one of his fiery explosions. At this rate she wasn't so sure turtles and nitroglycerin would last very long around one another.

Kicking off her shoes, Sabrina grabbed a box of tissues on her way to her rocking chair. Curling up on the seat, she wiped the first batch of tears away. She should have known there would be trouble, not only with Guy but with Brad. He was a veritable volcano of emotions while she, by comparison, was an emotionally barren desert—not the best of combinations.

Which left her where? With the memory of Brad's kisses that afternoon, his sharing with her, and then his accusations and anger. He'd even had the nerve to call her Golden Girl again, a deliberate attempt on his part to hurt her. He'd succeeded. What a mess.

Another wave of tears filled her eyes. "Men stink!" she declared. "Not you," she assured Thomas, who'd just jumped onto her lap to comfort her.

The cat sympathetically licked her cheek.

"Thanks," she sniffed. "I needed that."

Brad was in a rotten mood—had been all day. Or so everyone else informed him, including his sister, Helen, who'd stopped by during her lunch hour to show him her photos of Cancun. He zipped through all four packets of prints in less than two minutes flat.

Helen hadn't been pleased, but then neither was he. After all, she'd been relaxing on some sunny beach while he'd been coping with family traumas, among other things.

"You didn't even look at them," Helen protested as he stuffed the last batch back into the envelope.

"I've got better things to do." Brad was irritated and he made no attempt to hide that fact. But then he had never been one to disguise his feelings much, a trait that apparently threw someone with the highbrow restraint of Sabrina. Well, it was certainly too late to change him now, and he resented anyone trying.

"Excuse me for being alive," Helen retorted.

"Do you have any idea of what went on while you were living it up in Mexico?"

"Mom said that Grandmother left Granddad, and that he had to woo her back," Helen replied. "I wish I'd been here to see that!"

"I wish you'd been here, too. Then *you* could have handled it."

"What's the problem? From all I've heard, you did a great job. You and Sabrina Stewart. Grandmother told me you have a thing for her."

"I do not have a thing for her," Brad denied, even though he did. "Is nothing sacred in this family?" he growled.

"Very little. You should know that by now."

"Isn't there someplace else you have to be?" he inquired pointedly.

"All right, already. I'm leaving. See if I ever show you my photographs again," Helen said in a huffy tone. "Just remember that if it hadn't been for me, you wouldn't even have met up with your precious Sabrina Stewart again."

"Don't do me any more favors, okay?"

"Aha," Helen said knowingly. "Now I get it. You two had a fight."

Brad pointedly aimed his finger at the door. "Go."

It seemed to Brad that Helen had barely left his office when his secretary buzzed him with the news that his grandfather was outside. Great. Brad could see he was going to get tons of work done today. He had yet to even start going through the pile of applications on his desk for the opening that had to be filled on his work crew.

"Young people these days," Joseph grumbled as he entered Brad's office. "Would you believe I saw some punk toss his cigarette butt right onto the sidewalk? Do you know how long it takes a cigarette butt to decompose? Thirty years. I learned that from Sabrina," Joseph confessed.

Brad had learned plenty from Sabrina, too. Learned what she *really* thought of him—that he was some redneck who went around punching people for the fun of it. She and her family might not be wealthy now, but they still had a strange set of standards that he didn't understand.

"I don't want to talk about Sabrina," Brad stated. "What are you doing down here in town today, anyway?"

"Sabrina is recording our voices for the video tape at Memories today. We were early so we stopped by the waterfront first. Your grandmother is shopping. But what do you mean you don't want to talk about Sabrina? You two have a fight or something?"

"Or something. I walked in last night and found some guy manhandling her."

"I hope you knocked his lights out," Joseph forcefully declared.

"Of course I did. And Sabrina is mad at me for it. Does that makes sense to you? I come to her defense, yet somehow I end up being the bad guy. But I don't want to talk about it."

"You're trying to tell me that Sabrina is mad at you because you punched some guy who was forcing his attentions on her?"

"That's right."

"What's wrong with her?"

"Beats me."

"Who was the guy?"

"Guy Smut-Jones," Brad replied, using his own adaptation of Guy's name.

"Oh, him," Joseph said, dismissing Guy as if he were of no more importance than a cockroach. "That's the one you got into a lot of fights with as a kid, isn't it?"

"That's the one."

"You won the fight, didn't you?"

"It wasn't even a fight," Brad replied. "I decked the guy with one blow. He never laid a hand on me."

"Good going!" Joseph said warmly.

"Sabrina didn't think so."

Joseph shrugged. "You know how women are. Strange. She'll get over it, you'll see. When we go over there, I'll talk to her..."

"No, you won't."

"Okay, I'll have your grandmother do it."

"Absolutely not. You're not to say a word," Brad said vehemently. "Not a word. Got that?"

"Whatever you say. Nice painting," Joseph noted, with an approving nod at Violet's watercolor, which was now framed and hanging in a place of honor next to Brad's stuffed fish.

Brad didn't trust his grandfather's change of subject for one minute. "I mean it, Granddad. Don't talk to Sabrina."

"She's going to think it's a little strange if I show up and don't say a word," Joseph retorted humorously. "I'm supposed to be there to talk so she can record me."

"You know what I mean."

"You worry too much. Just relax. Everything will work out fine. Look at your grandmother and me."

"How's everything going with you two, anyway?" Brad asked.

"Fine," Joseph replied. "Better than fine. Great. Like we're on our second honeymoon."

"Good. I'm glad."

"Now about you and Sabrina—"

"Granddad..." Brad said warningly.

"All right, all right. Mum's the word. How about those Cubs?"

Sabrina longed for a bag of cheese curls. That or a long vacation. Her eyes still felt red and scratchy from her crying jag the other night. She'd refused to allow herself to cry yesterday and had prevented it from happening by keeping frantically busy all day—doing her spring cleaning two seasons late, since it was now September and almost officially fall. She hadn't shed a tear all day. Instead she'd ended up crying in her sleep, a dirty trick for her psyche to play on her in her opinion.

And all right—in her more lucid moments she was willing to admit that it still hurt that Brad had accused her of leading Guy on. She still wondered if Brad and Guy had even been fighting over her at all, or if she'd just been some kind of trophy they'd both been vying over. And she worried that Guy might make trouble for Brad.

Talking to Eliot partly reassured her on that last count. She'd told him everything first thing that morning.

"So Brad hit him, hmm?" Eliot murmured.

"I'm sorry," Sabrina said.

Her words obviously surprised Eliot. "You are?"

"I don't want the incident to reflect badly on you or this company."

"And according to what you said earlier, you also don't want Brad getting into trouble," Eliot added perceptively.

"That's right. Guy was making all kinds of threats when he walked out of here."

"He's lucky he still could walk and that Brad didn't break both his legs."

Now Sabrina was the one who was surprised. "You approve of what Brad did?"

"Not necessarily, but I can understand why he did it. I'd heard that there was no love lost between him and Guy. As for what happened here Saturday night, I wouldn't worry about Guy. I doubt that he's going to brag about getting knocked on his royal behind by Brad. However, I plan on doing some damage control myself just in case Guy tries making any accusations against you or this firm. I'll make sure our reputation remains clear," Eliot assured her.

"How do you plan on doing that?"

"All it takes are a few subtle comments in the right ears."

"That's what I'm afraid Guy will do," Sabrina said.

"Those ears no longer listen to Guy and he doesn't have the intelligence to even realize it. Don't worry about a thing."

Easier said than done, Sabrina realized.

"So what's this about you and my grandson having a fight?" Joseph demanded the moment he saw Sabrina.

"Joseph, you weren't supposed to say anything," Violet reprimanded him.

"I'm too old to go pussyfooting around," Joseph retorted.

"Did Brad ask you to talk to me?" Sabrina inquired.

"He ordered me not to talk to you. I asked him how I was supposed to do a recording if I wasn't allowed to talk to you. I also mentioned that thing you told me about cigarette butts taking thirty years to decompose. He didn't seem real impressed, though," Joseph noted. "I think he was in a bad mood."

So am I, Sabrina wanted to say. Instead she stuck to business, handing Joseph a script she'd done up. "I've written down some excerpts from our interviews for you to read aloud in the recording booth and then I'll dub them over the appropriate sections of the video portion of the tape."

"Fine, but what are you going to do about Brad?" Joseph asked.

"Joseph," Violet warned.

"Don't tell me it's none of my business," he retorted. "Matchmaking was none of their business but Sabrina and Brad did it anyway and we're glad they did, so that gives us the right to butt into their business the same way they did ours."

"You could just be making the situation worse," Violet said.

"They're not even talking to each other. What could get worse than that? You're not planning on ducking out of your invitation to our anniversary party, are you, Sabrina?" Joseph demanded suspiciously.

"Well, I..." Sabrina had been tempted to cancel in view of the fight she'd had with Brad. She thought it would make it less awkward all the way around.

"It would really mean a lot to us both if you'd come, my dear," Violet said. "It wouldn't be the same without you. In fact, there wouldn't even be a party if it hadn't been for you."

Sabrina couldn't refuse the pleading look in Violet's vibrant blue eyes. "I'll be there," she promised.

"Good." Violet beamed. "I'm so glad that's settled. Now we won't talk about anything else that's stressful for the time being. Just tell us what you want us to do for this recording."

All things considered, Sabrina thought she'd sidestepped the issue of Brad rather well. But after the recording session, which thankfully had gone smoothly, Sabrina realized she might have congratulated herself too soon as Violet gently pulled her aside just before leaving.

"You go ahead, Joseph," Violet instructed her husband. "I just wanted to discuss something briefly with Sabrina."

"Hope you can talk some sense into her," Joseph stated. "I'll be waiting in the car for you."

"Subtlety is not in the vocabulary of the men in this family," Violet ruefully told Sabrina. "Putting their foot in their mouth *is* a family trait, however. I'm sorry if Joseph upset you. Brad gave him express orders not to discuss any of this with you."

"Brad told his grandfather what happened?"

Violet nodded.

"And I suppose Joseph approved of Brad's behavior?"

Again, Violet nodded.

"What about you?" Sabrina asked.

"I approve of a man protecting the woman he cares about. But I don't think that's what upset you about Brad's behavior, is it?"

"No. It was the intensity of his reaction. He looked angry enough to kill someone."

"Were you afraid that Brad would hurt you?" Violet asked.

"Not really. I thought he'd break Guy's jaw, though."

"And that bothers you."

"It bothers me that Guy and Brad were fighting over me as if I were some kind of trophy—although Brad insisted on reminding me that it wasn't a fight at all, bragging about the way he'd knocked down Guy without getting hit himself. Not that I wanted Brad to get hit, that's not it at all. It's just... I don't know." Sabrina rubbed her forehead, where another headache was making itself felt. "It's hard to explain."

"They're men, my dear," Violet stated humorously. "You can't expect them to be logical."

"Brad certainly wasn't being logical. He actually had the nerve to ask me if I'd been leading Guy on."

"And that hurt you, didn't it?"

Sabrina nodded.

"But you must remember that Bradley was hurting, too, my dear. I doubt that he really thought you'd done anything wrong."

"He treated me as if I were an idiot!"

Violet patted Sabrina's shoulder understandingly. "As I said before, the men in my family do have a way of putting their foot in their mouths."

"He accused me of wanting a lapdog," Sabrina continued. "I just wanted him to be reasonable. There's got to be a middle ground between a raving caveman and a lapdog. Brad stormed into that room with both fists going."

"You would have preferred that he hadn't gotten so angry? That he'd stayed calm?"

"Yes."

"Ah, but telling Bradley to stay calm is like telling a dog not to bark. My grandson is an emotional man."

"So I've noticed."

"I think perhaps that's one of the reasons why you noticed him in the first place," Violet suggested.

"Brad is hard to ignore," Sabrina agreed. "Especially when he's knocking someone senseless at your feet. He said the bad blood between himself and Guy went way back. I sometimes wonder if I was just an excuse for Brad to be able to punch Guy."

"I know that Guy and his crowd gave Brad a lot of trouble when they were both younger, but if Brad wanted to punch Guy he's had plenty of opportunity before you came back to town. They haven't argued since they were teenagers. As for what you said earlier—about being a trophy—I'll admit that the Romanovski men tend to be possessive. But only about someone they care about. Are you waiting for Bradley to apologize?"

"I have a feeling I'd have a long wait," Sabrina replied.

Violet nodded her agreement. "It's male pride, you see."

What about my pride? Sabrina wanted to ask. After all, she was the one who'd been pawed by Guy and yelled at by Brad.

"I wouldn't presume to give you advice," Violet said. "I know how much I hated being told what to do when I left Joseph. All I will say is that you should consider that my grandson acted out of concern for you. Now it's up to you. Just listen to your heart."

Listen to your heart? Ah, but that was part of the problem right there. Sabrina's heart was as confused as the rest of her!

The day of the anniversary party, Sabrina spent most of the morning and the entire afternoon getting ready for the party, which didn't even start until seven that evening. Having long since progressed beyond nervous, she was now well on her way to sheer panic.

Why had she agreed to go? She should have bowed out gracefully. How was she supposed to face Brad? What was she supposed to say to him? Would he even speak to her? Was he bringing another woman to the party? What would she do if he did? The questions kept battering away at her brain like persistent woodpeckers. Unfortunately no answers came to the rescue.

The engraved invitation had said that the attire would be formal. That really only left her with one choice—the electric blue evening gown was the only formal gown she still owned. It was full-length and glittery, but not gaudy or ostentatious. It would do.

Before she slipped the dress on, she gave herself the full beauty treatment—including a long soak in a hot tub filled with her favorite bath oil, one she used sparingly these days due to the exorbitant price of replacing it. She'd considered using peel-on nails to hide the two she'd ripped handling the video camera the day before, but had been forced to ditch that plan when the sticky nails stuck to all the wrong places. No doubt the fact that her fingers were trembling at the time had added to the problem.

Her hair, too, had taken longer than normal to do, but it had finally cooperated and was now pinned up in a stylish chignon. Her makeup was done to perfection, if she did say so herself. She was even wearing new underwear, a matching bra-and-panty set in sky blue. Yes, she'd done everything possible to boost her self-confidence.

Despite all that, Sabrina almost turned back twice on her way to the country club where the private party was being held. But she'd made a promise and she couldn't renege on it now. So she took her courage and her matching blue-beaded purse in hand and walked into the country club's elegant foyer with dignity and grace. Or so she hoped.

Violet and Joseph were at the door of the ballroom to greet her. "I'm so glad you came," Violet said before hugging her.

The older woman's warm welcome touched her deeply. Sabrina hurriedly blinked away the faint prickle of tears behind her eyes, but not before Violet had seen the telltale shimmer.

"Are you okay?" Violet asked worriedly.

"I'm fine," Sabrina said. "You look lovely." The icy blue dress Violet wore matched the vibrant color of her eyes to perfection, while the style showed off the older woman's trim figure.

"Thank you, my dear," Violet replied. "You look lovely, too."

"Wait till you see Brad in his monkey suit. He looks more uncomfortable in his tuxedo than I do in mine. I don't know why Violet made us wear these dumb things," Joseph grumbled.

"Brad looks dashing and so do you," Violet retorted. "Sabrina, my dear, I'd like to introduce you to Brad's parents—Joe Junior and his wife Carol."

Sabrina wondered if Brad had told his parents anything about her. They were looking at her with undisguised curiosity. As if answering her silent question, Brad's father said, "We've heard a lot about you."

Sabrina then wondered if what he'd heard had been good or bad, but she lacked the nerve to inquire.

"We certainly have," Brad's mother concurred. "We all watched the family-chronicle video tape last night and were very impressed. You did a wonderful job on it."

"Thank you," Sabrina replied. "I'm glad everyone enjoyed it."

"It turned out even better than I thought it would," Joseph said. "That music at the beginning of the tape was the New World Symphony by Dvořák."

"So you told us last night, Dad," Joe Junior said with an indulgent smile.

"Dvořák was Czech, not Polish, but he wrote some good stuff, anyway," Joseph continued. "Did I tell you that Brad picked it out? Told me he hummed a few bars to Sabrina, and she was able to identify it. I never knew my grandson could hum part of a symphony. How about that?"

Sabrina remembered the occasion well. Brad had covered any self-consciousness he may have felt by making an impatient demand for her to "name this tune." She wondered if that was how he covered up other signs of uncertainty, by masking it in confidence and storming on ahead. The idea of Brad being uncertain was an unfamiliar one, one she'd never considered before. She didn't have long to consider it now, either, as Joseph's voice interrupted her introspection.

"I liked the big band stuff the best, though," Joseph admitted. "Give me Benny Goodman or Glen Miller music any day. The band is going to play some of those great tunes later for our dancing enjoyment. I've been told I'm quite light on my feet."

"I told him that," Violet said.

"It's true, isn't it?"

Violet patted her husband's arm. "Of course, dear."

"Save a space on your dance card for me, Sabrina—if Brad will let me cut in, that is. Ouch! Now what did I say?" Joseph demanded, rubbing the arm Violet had just socked.

"Why nothing, dear," Violet innocently replied.

"Oh, I get it." Joseph nodded judiciously. "Right. Maybe we should talk about the environment or something."

"Violet's got me cutting those rings around six-packs," Brad's mother hurriedly inserted. "She said you taught her a lot about recycling, Sabrina."

"Sabrina's taught me a lot—period," Violet stated.

"Violet's taught me a lot, too," Sabrina said slowly. She was only now realizing how much the older woman *had* taught her—important lessons about relationships and going after what you wanted. But then Violet had the advantage of being a very warm and loving woman. Sabrina didn't see herself that way at all. However, the older woman's example of doing something about a situation she was unhappy with did apply here.

Because it was certainly true that Sabrina was unhappy with the way things currently stood with Brad. She couldn't leave things as they were. She didn't know what the future would bring, she just knew she couldn't continue on this way. Granted there were a lot of problems, not least of which was Sabrina's fear of her own inability to emotionally love someone. Meanwhile there was Brad—a man positively seething with emotions.

Maybe, she realized with sudden insight, that was one of the reasons that Brad's punching Guy had upset her so much. His intensely emotional display of anger had served to reemphasize the differences between their personalities—he, so deeply emotional, she so judiciously dispassionate. Perhaps she'd been wrong to come down on him so hard. Violet was right, telling Brad to stay calm was like telling a dog not to bark. It was an inherent part of his nature. She couldn't change him. Did she really want to?

She certainly didn't have all the answers. But she was coming to realize one thing—she wanted Brad in her life.

A squeeze on her hand brought Sabrina back to the present.

"Courage, my dear," Violet whispered as she kissed her cheek. "You can do it."

"Do what?" Sabrina whispered back, eager for more words of wisdom.

"Whatever is necessary," Violet replied, giving her a reassuring hug.

Feeling appropriately fortified, Sabrina returned the hug before leaving Violet and Joseph to their other guests. If she wanted Brad, she'd have to go after him. She looked around the room and saw him standing by a potted plant, looking devilishly handsome in his black tuxedo. His white shirt was very conservative, no frills, and his bow tie was plain black.

Seeing him, after having been parted from him for almost a week, removed any trace of lingering doubt from Sabrina's mind. She'd missed him terribly. Looking at him now, she knew she felt more for Brad than she ever had for anyone else in her life. The time had come to let Brad know.

But how? She couldn't very well just walk up to him and announce her feelings, especially not after the fight they'd had.

"Hi, I'm Helen...Brad's sister. You must be Sabrina. I've been dying to meet you."

"You have?" Sabrina looked at the bubbly blonde in surprise.

"Absolutely. Don't look now, but Brad is glaring at us. Probably worrying that I'm going to spill the beans about some deep dark secret of his. Since anyone with half a brain can see that he's crazy about you, I don't think that there are really any dark secrets left to spill," Helen said, before adding, "you two had a fight, didn't you?"

Sabrina wasn't accustomed to such forthrightness on such short acquaintance. She stalled for time, trying to think of a polite way of avoiding that question.

"It's okay," Helen said. "You don't have to answer that. I didn't mean to make you feel uncomfortable. My big brother is probably already making you feel uncomfortable enough as it is. He didn't bring a date with him, just in case you were wondering," Helen added. "Oh-oh, I can see him giving me the evil eye again. I'd better be moving along. Just wanted to meet you for myself. Have a good time at the party and be sure to try the *kolackis* on the dessert table. They're made from a recipe that's been in the family for years. My great-grandmother brought it over with her from Poland—the recipe, not the *kolackis*," Helen noted with a laugh. With a cheery smile she left as quickly as she'd arrived.

If Brad were a thunderstorm, Sabrina noted, then his sister was a whirlwind. Already the noise level of a ballroom full of Romanovskis was boisterously loud. She was introduced to both sets of Brad's uncles and aunts as well as what seemed like at least twenty cousins.

Everyone seemed to be having a wonderful time. Everyone except for her...and possibly Brad. She did indeed catch him looking at her on more than one occasion. Even though he'd deliberately turned away without so much as a smile or a nod of recognition, she'd seen something in his eyes—a certain flare of hunger, a brooding passion that stiffened her resolve.

He obviously did not plan on making this easy on her. But he wouldn't make it impossible. She just had to make the first move...male pride being what it was.

The band had already begun doing its thing, playing big band hits from the thirties and forties. As soon as they reached a number that Sabrina recognized as being slow, she cranked up her nerve and decided to ask Brad to dance with her. After all, just about everyone else in the room was already dancing. It was the perfect opportunity, precisely what she'd been waiting for.

She'd just walk right up to him and...

Sabrina got that far before her voice deserted her. Brad stood there looking at her and not saying a word. But something about the *way* that he looked at her gave her courage. Now that she was closer to him there was no mistaking the smoldering eloquence of his eyes. They told her all she needed to know.

"Dance with me?" she invited softly.

He didn't say yes or no, but he did take her in his arms. He held her distantly, though, with courteous politeness, as if she were his maiden aunt. She slipped her hand from his shoulder to his shirtfront. It was cheating she knew, but she needed to check out his heartbeat.

To her relief it was not as sedate as his dancing style would indicate. She could feel the throbbing beat beneath her fingertips. With satisfaction she noticed the increased tempo as her fingers tiptoed their way across his chest.

"What do you think you're doing?" Brad growled.

"Dancing with you?" she replied innocently enough. "Why? Aren't I doing it right?"

"Like living dangerously, do you?"

Before Sabrina could think up a suitable answer to that one, the music ended and Brad whisked her out a pair of nearby French doors onto the deserted terrace.

She didn't have time to say a word before his mouth engulfed hers with unmistakable hunger. Deciding that words were a useless means of communication anyway, she abandoned them in favor of other means of expression. She melted against him with a fluid and feverish desire that she made no attempt to disguise. Then she returned his kiss with all her heart, letting him know how much she'd missed him.

Fueled by her response and his passion, their kiss became a sultry combination of dipping tongues and slanting mouths—a blend that left Sabrina breathless. She didn't care. She needed to keep kissing him more than she needed air. He made her want things she hadn't wanted in a long time, made her feel things she hadn't felt in a lifetime.

His lips sought hers again and again, as if he couldn't get enough of the taste of her. She certainly knew she felt the same way about him. She would have begrudged the short periods of time when his lips left hers to bestow a sexy string of kisses from her ear to her throat, had his mouth not felt delicious on her bare skin as well.

His hands also felt delicious as he molded her to him, his hands cupping the small of her back as he lifted her against him. Her hands had slipped beneath his tuxedo jacket and were spread out across his back, her fingers curling in delight and wrinkling the crispness of his white shirt.

The catlike movements drove Brad to distraction. His blood was burning, his mind reeling as he moved against her. Their embrace escalated until it reached the point where Brad had to break away or make love to her right there on the terrace!

"Come home with me tonight," Brad murmured roughly.

To his surprise and delight, Sabrina whispered her agreement.

Brad didn't wait a second longer. He hustled her out of the ballroom so fast Sabrina barely had the chance to say good-night to Violet and Joseph.

At any other time she would have felt bad about bending the rules of social protocol and leaving early, but Sabrina wasn't herself tonight. She was some dreamy-eyed girl for whom fantasies could come true and for whom all things were possible. She was Cinderella, glittering with stardust and possessing the best kind of magic.

Although Brad made the drive to his place in record time, just a tad of the magic had worn off and a touch of awkwardness had taken its place as Sabrina followed him into his apartment.

She'd underestimated Brad's sensitivity, however. Instead of hauling her straight into the bedroom, he turned on the discreetly recessed lighting in the living room.

"Feel like dancing?" he inquired.

Sabrina nodded. She'd only had that one dance with him, after all. The music he put on was soulful and sexy. Holding out his hand to her, he slowly pulled her to him.

Ballroom dancing this wasn't! A sheet of paper couldn't have fit between them. They moved as one, swaying to the tempting beat.

Sabrina had never danced like this before in her life, but Brad inspired her. His fingers were threaded through hers, his other hand temptingly warm on the base of her spine as he held her close to him. His knee slid between hers as he guided her, slowly but surely, in the dance of seduction.

As the female singer throatily sang about her vision of love, Sabrina and Brad were acting out its promise. She slipped her arms around his neck. He held her to him, his fingertips spanning the tantalizing distance from the small of her back to the curve of her derriere. Her body brushed his with a constancy that was intimately pleasurable for them both.

There was dancing and then there was *dancing*. This was almost like making love standing up, Sabrina noted. So it came as no surprise to her that before the song had ended, she'd slid Brad's jacket from his shoulders and he'd started undoing the zip on her dress.

They were merely swaying in place now, and the way his body was moving against hers created a powerfully erotic friction that heated Sabrina's blood and evaporated any trace of awkwardness. Pagan emotions took over, freeing her, giving her the courage to slip the bow tie from Brad's shirt. The studs on his dress shirt were next and she managed those with a skillful ease she'd never have expected of herself.

Now that his shirt was open, the bare warmth of his skin caressed the length of her arms when she once again slid them around his neck. As the song neared the end, he dipped her backward, kissing the curve of her throat all the way up to her ear. By the time the singer crooned her last note about realizing love's dream, Brad had swung Sabrina up into his arms.

Laughing in delight, she kissed him as he carried her into his bedroom, to finish what they'd started. The stereo played on, but now they were making their own music. Brad set her back on her feet, letting her slide against the length of his body as he did so. It was a body Sabrina was coming to know very well, but wanted to know better—the throbbing warmth, the sturdy power, the shuddering response to her lightest touch.

Desire gave her a boldness she'd never had before. She acted on those needs, slipping his shirt away and baring him from the waist up. The muted light in his bedroom shimmered off his golden skin. It would have been a crime to have had any hair covering this chest, she noted dreamily. It was an artist's dream of symmetry and strength. She smoothed her hands over every tempting inch, from the powerful width of his shoulders to the taut plane of his stomach.

Brad seemed equally appreciative of her body as he lowered the zip of her dress even more. Now there was nothing but the tip of her shoulders and the curve of her breasts keeping the dress from sliding clear off. He seemed fascinated by this phenomenon, judging from the way his fingers brushed the creamy flesh revealed by her deeply cut bra.

Her cleavage held a particular interest for him as he devilishly drew one finger down its shadowy valley. His movements dislodged the last hold her dress had. It slid to her waist in an instant.

Brad caught his breath at the sight of her standing before him. The bra she was wearing—a tiny bit of wire and lace—displayed more than it covered. He gently cupped her with both hands, loving the feel of the silky lingerie beneath his palms. Knowing she would feel even silkier without it, he undid the bra. Freed from restraint, her breasts eagerly thrust forward, right into his waiting hands.

Sabrina moaned with growing pleasure as he caressed her softly and seductively. The feel of his thumb tenderly brushing the tip of her breast made her shiver with delight. Bending her backward over his arm, he lowered his mouth to the creamy mounds, further seducing her with a swirl of his tongue. The excitement was so intense she thought her knees would buckle.

As if sensing her unsteadiness, Brad swept her up in his arms again and carried her the few feet to his bed. When he lowered her to it, Sabrina was surprised to feel shifting movement beneath her instead of the solidness of a mattress. Startled she tightened her hold on him, which sent him toppling down onto her.

The shifting movement intensified. "You've got a water bed!" she exclaimed unsteadily.

"Yes." Brad rolled over so that she was atop him, providing her with a steady anchor should she need one. "Don't tell me you get seasick on a water bed?"

"No. It was just a surprise, that's all."

"I'm *surprised* we still have this many clothes on." He lowered the dress's zip even further, clear down to the base of her spine. This was familiar territory, territory he'd explored during their intimate dance. But she felt so much better to him without the barrier of her evening dress getting in his way.

Lying as she was, on top of Brad, Sabrina could feel her breasts pressed against his bare chest. She sinuously rubbed against him and was rewarded by him trailing his fingers from her nape clear down to the slope of her bottom, where a pair of silky panties got in his way. But not for long.

Sabrina nibbled on his ear, whispering her pleasure at the provocative sweep of his hands. The long hypnotic strokes were infinitely tempting. With his help, she shimmied out of her dress, which fell to the floor in a pool of electric blue. His tuxedo pants soon joined her dress there.

The anticipation was building as he took her in his arms once more. His kisses were like contained lightning, flickering across her skin and across her soul—filling her heart and mind with their erotic illumination. The thunder was provided by their combined heartbeats. The few bits of clothing separating them were soon swept away as if they'd never existed.

This was the way they were meant to be, Sabrina hazily realized. No barriers, nothing between his heart and hers but the warmth of their bare skin. The tempo picked up as the urgency of their need increased with every stroke, every caress.

Brad's tempting fingers were coming ever closer to the one spot that was aching for his attention. Touching her there, he coaxed her into revealing her innermost fantasies, thrilling her with the butterfly-soft contact, shifting his hand and setting up a rhythm that soon had her steeped with passion.

Just when Sabrina thought she couldn't stand the spiraling excitement a moment later, he rolled away from her. When she realized he was taking care of their protection, her smile turned sultry. She received him back with open arms as he came to her, filling her aching emptiness and completing their union with one final surge of motion.

She closed around him in a rippling welcome that was as elemental as time itself. Her gasps of joy matched his heated groan. Sabrina looked into Brad's eyes, but the sliding rush of his thrusts created such a powerful storm within her that her lids fluttered closed as the first flutters of delight struck her.

Her universe expanded and contracted—the tiny ripples growing into surging waves as she absorbed him into her very soul. Floating in that higher plane, Sabrina felt Brad stiffen in her arms as he, too, reached that magical moment.

When it was all over, she held him in her arms once again. Only now did she notice the sensual smoothness of satin sheets beneath her naked body. Snuggling against Brad, she languidly whispered, "Now that I've learned how to fly, when is my first swimming lesson?"

Ten

Brad knew Sabrina was talking about more than just swimming lessons. She was talking about trust. Finally.

"I love you," he murmured, surprising himself at first. While Brad knew he'd felt the emotion, he hadn't expected the words to slip out now. Not that he had any reason to keep them to himself—that wasn't his way. He'd just planned on working up to the declaration, instead of blurting it out as he had.

"Oh, Brad..." Her voice caught.

"It's not a very fancy way to say it, I know—"

She placed her trembling fingers to his lips. "I don't know what to say."

He kissed her fingertips. "That's easy. Tell me you love me, too," he gently prompted her.

But it wasn't easy. Not for Sabrina.

Brad saw that. "Unless you *don't* love me," he growled, his good mood disappearing.

She had to say something. So she told him the truth. "I'm not sure I'm capable of loving someone."

"What are you talking about?" he said impatiently. "If you were any more capable, I'd have died of pleasure."

Sabrina blushed. "I don't mean physically capable. I mean emotionally capable."

Brad pulled away from her. "If this is your way of saying you don't feel the same way about me, stop mincing words and get to the point."

She'd hurt him, something she'd tried so hard to avoid. Should she have lied and just said the words? But would it be a lie? She'd never felt this way toward anyone else. But was it love? How was she supposed to know?

"Brad, if I could love anyone it would be you."

He could hear the torment in her voice. "Then what's stopping you?"

"It's a long story."

"I'm not going anywhere."

"You're not?"

"No." He brushed the back of his hand across her cheek. "I'm a Romanovski. We may get angry but we don't give up so easily, remember?" Now that he'd gotten over his initial shock, Brad realized that something else was at work here. A woman like Sabrina didn't jump into bed with a man just because she was attracted to him, she'd told him so herself. He'd seen the look in her eyes; that hadn't just been passion. It had been more. Why was she so reluctant to admit it?

"Come here." He took her back in his arms, settling her on his chest. "Now tell me why you think you can't love someone."

"Because it isn't a feeling I can remember ever having experienced. Not even as a child."

"Surely your parents..."

Sabrina shook her head. "It's not their fault," she said hurriedly. "They're just not emotional people. And neither am I."

"Bull." Brad's colorful commentary indicated his disagreement. "I don't buy that."

"I'm not selling anything."

"You're selling yourself short if you think you're not an emotional woman. Okay, so maybe you keep your emotions more to yourself than some people do, but that doesn't mean those emotions aren't there. Come on. If you're so emotionless, why did you take in a stray kitten and keep it even after it grew into a monster cat?"

"That's different."

"Is it? Would your parents have done something like that?"

"No."

"I rest my case. You're not like your parents."

"It's not that simple." Her long story had been boiled down to a few bare bones. They didn't tell the whole story: the years of distancing herself from others, her failure at being able to emotionally commit to someone, her gradual acceptance that she was somehow lacking in that regard. Closeness didn't come easily for her. "I'm not like you."

He trailed a caressing finger over her heart. "I noticed."

"I wasn't talking about that!" She didn't push his hand away, however. How could she when what he was doing felt so good?

"Don't you think we've talked enough?" he murmured against her lips. "We seem to communicate just fine this way..."

His kiss was intended to distract her and it did. But not for long.

"You're sure you're not angry with me?" she whispered.

"Does it feel as if I'm angry with you?" he huskily countered.

"I wish things were different. I wish *I* were different."

"I kinda like you the way you are."

"You're a warm and wonderfully emotional man. You deserve better."

"Me?" Brad smoothed her hair away from her face, letting his fingers linger in the silky softness. "I've got you in my arms and that's enough for now."

"It's just that... I wish I could say the words..."

"The words aren't that important. The feeling is." Before kissing her, he whispered, "Just let yourself feel, Sabrina."

And she did. The physical feelings weren't the problem, however—the inner emotions were. And those were a complicated mess of conflicting messages with multiple threads of thought getting caught up and knotted all together.

"You're thinking too much," Brad murmured against her lips. "Stop it or I'll be forced to take drastic measures."

"Like what?"

"Like this...." He kissed his way from her fingertips to her wrist, past the juncture of her elbow, clear to her shoulder, then over to her bare collarbone. It was a devilishly circuitous route to his ultimate destination, the creamy slopes of her breasts.

Spearing her fingers through his dark hair, Sabrina held him to her as he delighted her with the provocative stabs of his tongue. His seduction was skillful and guaranteed to capture her complete attention. By the time he lifted his head she was intoxicated with passion.

"Ever wonder who put the naughty in nautical?" he inquired with a wicked grin.

"You did," she returned saucily, rolling him over so that she was perched atop him.

Brad felt the silky strands of her hair brushing his chest as she moved over him, kissing him with bewitching hunger. Brad's last coherent thought was that even if Sabrina didn't realize it yet—this classy, incredibly sexy lady *did* love him. He was sure of it. And he planned on doing everything in his power to make *her* sure of it, too.

Sabrina's swimming lessons were a huge success—as far as Brad was concerned, anyway. Any excuse to have her in his arms was worthwhile in his book. And they were both learning something—she the breaststroke, and he how delectably her rear end wiggled as she scissor-kicked. The red swimsuit she thought was modest actually hugged her body with an enviable faithfulness to every single curve.

"Brad!" Sabrina sputtered, after his wandering hands and attention distracted her so much that she ended up swallowing a mouthful of chlorinated water. "I thought we agreed that you were going to concentrate on these swimming lessons."

"I am concentrating. Can't you tell?"

"You're distracting me!"

"All I was doing was holding you afloat," he protested innocently.

"How am I ever going to learn how to do the breaststroke when you keep stroking my breast?" she demanded.

"My hand slipped."

"That's what you said last time."

"All right, if that's the way you feel about it, then we'll practice the back float."

Sabrina dutifully lowered her feet to the bottom of the heated indoor pool. The water level was just above her breasts. She had no intention of getting in over her head—not in the literal sense. Figuratively speaking, she was *already* in way over her head with Brad, definitely swimming in what were uncharted waters for her. But so far she felt she was navigating fairly well, if she did say so herself.

Her swimming lessons were coming along fairly well, too. She'd quickly learned that the best way to keep her long hair out of her eyes was to plait it into a French braid that began at the top of her head and hung down to her shoulder blades. Brad had also developed a fondness for her wearing her hair this way—it was easier for him to lift out of his way so that he could nuzzle the creamy expanse of her bare skin. He was doing it again right now.

"Are you sure no one's watching?" Sabrina asked somewhat nervously.

"I told you, I rented the clubhouse for this hour. No one else is allowed in. Come on," he said briskly, switching from lover to instructor. "Back float. Time's a-wasting."

"Back float?" she repeated, needing more time to make the transition from fantasy to reality.

"That's right." Brad braced his hands in the middle of her back as she leaned backward in the water. She trusted him implicitly. While he might not be able to resist a caress here and there, he'd never given her cause to think he'd drop her or let her go to make it on her own. He was there for her, an encouraging presence, understanding that she'd let him know when she was ready to go it alone.

Sabrina still felt a little strange that first instant when her feet left the solid bottom of the pool and floated to the surface. She used her arms the way Brad had shown her.

Floating on her back, she looked up at him grinning down at her and couldn't help herself. Lifting her arms from the water, she reached for him. Her feet sank back down to the bottom as she slid her arms around his neck and kissed him.

Her action caught him by surprise—she could tell by the startled moment it took him to kiss her back. She made good use of the time, tempting him as he so often tempted her, with a provocative swipe of her tongue and a gentle nip with her teeth. His growl told her she'd aroused a tiger.

Tugging her closer, he hefted her up. She wrapped her legs around his waist. And still they kissed. Since they'd made love for the first time a few days ago, the desire between them had grown rather than diminished. It was a phenomenon that amazed Sabrina, when she was sane enough to think about it. This wasn't one of those moments. Sanity had given way to deep-seated need.

When Brad's lips finally did leave hers it was only for the tempting softness of her bare shoulders—where he slid first one, then the other strap of her swimsuit off her shoulders.

Through the passion-induced cloud fogging her mind, Sabrina heard the sound of approaching footsteps. Was someone there? she frantically wondered. She turned to see, whipping her head around so quickly that her braid flew, its damp tip almost smacking Brad right in the face.

"We're not alone," she exclaimed before hurriedly ducking behind him.

"Pool's closed!" Brad curtly informed the intruder, while protectively shielding Sabrina from view.

"Your hour's up!" a voice shouted back.

Brad's softly muttered curse was enough to turn the air blue.

"I guess that's all for this lesson," Sabrina noted with a rueful laugh.

"Easy for you to say." Brad released her, but he had to swim two quick laps before he was in any shape to get out of the pool.

Sabrina promised she'd make it up to him when they got home, and she did.

"I can't believe you made me throw that fish back," Brad muttered in disgust. They were in Sabrina's apartment several days later after having returned from their first—and if Sabrina had any say in it, their last—fishing excursion together. "A perfectly good and legal catch, yet you made me throw it back."

She refused to feel guilty. "The poor little thing couldn't breathe. It would have died if you hadn't put it back in the water."

"Sabrina, you don't seem to understand," he said with painstaking slowness. "The object of fishing is to catch the fish and keep it. *You* eat seafood. Fish die. It happens."

"Not in front of me, it doesn't," she stated. "I can't order live lobsters from a restaurant for the same reason. You might as well know that about me now."

"I certainly know not to take you fishing with me anymore."

"Al will probably be relieved," she noted with a grin, unable to feel any regret at not having to go along on future outings. "I think he prefers that you two guys fish alone, anyway—some sort of male-bonding ritual, no doubt. Which reminds me, I have something for you," she said in a soft and sultry voice. "Close your eyes. And no peeking."

Brad's imagination was working overtime as he conjured up a number of possibilities as to the surprise she had in store for him—his favorite involved Sabrina peeling off her clothes. If that were the case he sure didn't want to miss one second of the show.

"I saw that, buster," she exclaimed, catching him trying to steal a look.

To his disappointment, she was still fully dressed.

"Close those eyes again," she scolded, "or no surprise."

He reluctantly closed them.

"Okay, hold out your arms."

Now that sounded more promising to Brad. But instead of her warm body, he felt the crinkle of paper in his hands. Paper over something else.

"Okay, you can open your eyes now," Sabrina told him. "Go ahead, open it."

It was a fishing rod, the new one he'd been eyeing at the tackle shop for the past month.

"How did you know...?" Brad asked.

"I talked to Al. There's a card in there, too."

Brad opened the tiny envelope. On a classy white card Sabrina had written "From the one who got away." He was stunned.

"Did I surprise you?" she inquired.

Brad nodded slowly. "That's one way of putting it, yes." How could she have known? Surely Al hadn't spilled the beans about *that* as well as telling her the kind of fishing rod he wanted.

Sabrina could see Brad trying to put the pieces together. Taking pity on him, she said, "Remember that dinner we had with Al and his wife the other evening?"

Brad nodded.

"Remember how long Judy and I were in the ladies' room?"

Brad put the rest together himself. "She told you?"

It was Sabrina's turn to nod.

"And Al told her?"

Sabrina nodded again.

"I'll kill them both," he declared.

"Judy didn't reveal your little secret on purpose," Sabrina assured him. "It just sort of slipped out."

"Why didn't you tell me at the time?"

"I thought this was a more appropriate way of letting you know."

"You're not angry?"

"I know you better than you might think, Brad Romanovski," she informed him. "While a woman of lesser intelligence might easily take offense at being likened to a stuffed fish like the one hanging on your office wall, I on the other hand decided to be magnanimous and forgive you."

"You did, huh?"

"I did."

Brad carefully set the fishing rod aside. "Feeling pretty proud of yourself, aren't you?" he inquired.

She nodded. She had no doubt that if she'd heard about being labeled "the one that got away" earlier in her relationship with Brad, she would have been furious. And she would have had further cause to doubt his motives.

The difference now was that she *knew* he loved her. He hadn't said the words again, but he proved it to her in so many small ways—from the way he brushed her hair with gentle awkwardness to the way he'd taken her fishing simply because he'd wanted to be with her. She was even beginning to hope she could love him back. The kind of delicious optimism she'd been experiencing lately was heady stuff.

"It so happens that I have a surprise for you, too," Brad told her. "You'll have to fish it out of my back pocket." His smile was very male and very smug as he added, "Oh, but I forgot. You don't like to go fishing."

"Fishing in your pocket is infinitely more appealing than trying to steal little fishies from the ocean," she informed him archly. "Which pocket? Left or right?"

"That would be telling. You'll have to find out for yourself," he murmured.

Sabrina took him up on his invitation, sliding her hand into his pocket and mischievously enjoying a little seductive exploring along the way. His jeans fit so well that there wasn't much room in his pockets, but she creatively took advantage of what space there was before snaring the small article wrapped in tissue paper.

"What's this?" she asked.

"Open it and you'll find out," he replied.

Nestled in the wrinkled tissue paper were a delicate pair of earrings. They looked familiar to Sabrina.

"These are beautiful," she noted, touching the hand-enameled and raised gold finish. "And very unusual. I've seen these somewhere before." She frowned a second and then it came to her. The catalog from the Boston Museum of Fine Arts! She'd seen these in the catalog and had written a note in the margin "Someday."

She asked him the same question he'd asked her earlier. "How did you know?"

"I saw the catalog on your coffee table."

"These are replicas of fourth-century Roman earrings," she murmured in delight.

Brad shrugged. "I do know that the inscription says 'To the beautiful one,' and you are beautiful."

Sabrina threw her arms around him. "I don't know how to thank you."

"Yes, you do," he wickedly assured her.

Her laughter was bewitchingly inviting as she took him by the hand and led him to her bedroom. Once there, the gifts they exchanged were of the heart and the flesh. She showered him with kisses—first, the quick teasing kind and then the intimately promising ones. Brad matched her lavish generosity, slanting his mouth across her parted lips and engaging her tempting tongue in an erotic tussle.

The ensuing thrust and parry was a provocative prologue for what was yet to come. Sabrina wasn't exactly sure how their clothes disappeared with such gratifying speed, but she was glad they did. She melted against him, wanting to feel him against her, within her. Moments later she got what she wanted as he came to her with a tempestuous passion that took her breath away.

To Sabrina their lovemaking became a sultry storm with the lightning of satisfaction growing ever closer until it was right there—crashing over them in undulating bursts of ecstatic energy, consuming them both with its elemental force.

Exhausted but infinitely satisfied, Sabrina fell asleep with a very satisfied smile on her lips.

"Hey, did you know that your cat chases pistachio nut shells?" Brad called out to her from the kitchen the next morning.

It was Sunday and they were lounging around her apartment after having consumed a hefty number of waffles.

"Come here and watch this," Brad demanded.

Sabrina walked into the kitchen to find Thomas crouching low, ready to pounce.

"Okay," Brad said in a pseudo-announcer's voice. "I'm winding up for the pitch and it's a low slider."

Thomas fielded the throw with no trouble at all and immediately began chasing the nutshell as it sped across the floor, reminding Sabrina of Bambi on an ice pond. Only Thomas had the advantage of heading in two directions at once as his front end moved left while his rear end slid right.

Brad was leaning against the doorframe, holding his side as he laughed. "Look at the way his legs keep going around and around, yet he's not getting anywhere! He can't get any traction on this floor. Talk about spinning your wheels...." Brad had to pause as another bout of laughter seized him. "Reminds me of those *Roadrunner* cartoons. Now what's his problem?" Brad asked as the cat abruptly stalked away.

"You hurt his feelings by laughing at him. He's very sensitive about being laughed at."

Brad eyed her in disbelief. "You're kidding, right?"

"Absolutely not. I keep telling you, Thomas has a personality all his own. He's a highly intelligent being. The sound of the phone ringing bothers him, so he knocks it off the hook. That takes intelligence."

"Good thing he hasn't learned how to dial out yet, or you'd be in trouble."

"He has been known to step on a number or two in his time."

"Great," Brad noted dryly. "A cat that dials Fiji. Try explaining that one to the phone company."

"Even if Thomas does dial Fiji, at least you have the comfort of knowing he won't talk long," she teased him back.

"You think that cat knows how good he's got it here?"

"Thomas probably thinks he's doing me a favor."

"That's gratitude for you."

"My grandmother used to tell me that gratitude and a dime won't buy you a cup of coffee."

"Another sentimental type like your parents?"

Sabrina nodded. "She taught me a lot, though, before she died when I was ten."

"What did she teach you?"

"How to sit up straight and tuck my ankles under a chair like a proper lady, for one thing. She was a stickler for propriety."

"Ah, I wondered where you'd learned that little trick. So I have your grandmother to thank for that, hmm? Too bad I wasn't able to meet her. Maybe I'll get to meet your parents instead someday."

Sabrina suddenly became very busy wiping down a kitchen counter that was already sparkling clean. "They're in Costa Rica for the next year or so, working on rain forest conservation. I hear they're making great strides there."

"You hear from them often?"

"They always send me a card at Christmas." She returned the dishcloth to the sink. "Can we change the subject, please?"

"It still makes you uncomfortable, talking about them, doesn't it?"

"There's nothing to say."

"You're nothing like them," he reminded her.

"You don't know that. You've never met them."

"I know you. If you had children you'd fuss over them as much as you do Thomas—"

"I do not *fuss*," she protested.

"And you'd continue to worry about them long after they'd reached the age of twenty-one. You'd keep close track of them to make sure they were doing okay."

"You make me sound like a mother hen."

"No. Just a warm and loving woman. I'm hoping that if I keep telling you that often enough, you'll see yourself that way, too." Coming up behind her, he hooked his arms around her waist and leaned down to nuzzle her cheek. "Think that's possible?"

"Maybe."

He looped his fingers together within touching distance of the swell of her breasts. "Only maybe?"

She leaned back against him. "Mmm... quite possibly."

"That's better."

Better was indeed an apt word to describe how things were going between her and Brad, Sabrina dreamily reflected. Each time he held her in his arms, she felt better and better. She felt as if there might be hope for her after all.

She was still reflecting on that hope as she made the bed a few minutes later. It felt surprisingly right having Brad in her living room, padding around wearing nothing more than a pair of pajama bottoms. She was wearing the top to the same pajamas. It was an advantageous arrangement for both of them, she noted with a grin. She got to enjoy his bare chest and he got to whistle at her legs.

Yes, she'd definitely done the right thing in buying the men's pajamas in the first place. Keeping a pair at her place and a pair at his had also been a good idea. Left on his own, Brad's concept of nightwear was nothing at all or a pair of briefs and a T-shirt in a pinch. While he looked great either of those ways, he also looked incredibly sexy with the drawstring waistband deliciously dipping beneath his navel. Mmm, yes, very sexy indeed!

Sabrina's naughty thoughts were interrupted by the arrival of Thomas, who'd jumped on the bed to join in the Changing of the Sheets ceremony—one of his favorite rituals because he got to hide under the sheets as Sabrina tried to smooth them over the mattress.

In the living room, the sound of the intercom buzzer made Brad look up from the Sunday funny papers he was reading. It took him a second to realize that Sabrina probably couldn't hear the buzz since she was down the hall in the bedroom. Knowing she wasn't expecting anyone, he answered it himself, figuring someone had probably made a mistake. People pushed the wrong buzzer—it happened.

Hitting the speaker button, he said, "Who is it?"

"Is this Sabrina Stewart's apartment?" a male voice inquired.

"Who wants to know?" Brad demanded suspiciously.

"Her father."

Eleven

"Now don't panic," Brad told Sabrina as she spread a clean top sheet on the bed, "but your parents are on their way up."

"On their way up from where?"

"Downstairs."

"That's not funny," she reprimanded him.

"I'm serious."

She froze. "You are?"

Brad nodded.

Sabrina panicked. She wanted to put the sheet over her head and hide in bed. She wasn't ready for this yet! But the sound of someone knocking on the front door told her that her time was up.

"Here!" She frantically grabbed a shirt and shoved it at Brad. "Hurry and put this on."

He shoved it back at her. "It's yours!"

"Then put on this one." She handed him another shirt with one hand while attempting to tug on a pair of jeans with the other hand. Then she replaced the decidedly male pajama top she wore with a T-shirt. But it seemed as if the faster she tried to move, the slower she went. Now she knew how Thomas must have felt skidding across the kitchen floor.

"Be right there!" she called out as she rushed down the hallway. Belatedly realizing that she had her T-shirt on inside out, she quickly tugged it off. With her head temporarily caught in the folds of the T-shirt, she almost tripped over the cat, who had gone to investigate the noisy pounding on the front door before deciding to head for quieter territory. Highly insulted at having his paws nearly stepped on, Thomas stalked into the bedroom while Sabrina paused to catch her breath.

By the time she opened the door a second later, she had plastered what she hoped was a calm smile on her face. "Mom, Dad, what are you doing here?"

"Aren't you going to invite us in?" her father inquired.

"Of course." Sabrina stepped aside, only now realizing that she'd been blocking the entrance as if standing guard. "Come in."

"We were in the vicinity attending a symposium on acid rain and thought we'd stop by," her father said. "We're spending the night with friends here in town."

"I wish you'd let me know that you were coming," Sabrina said.

"We didn't know ourselves until the last minute," her father replied. "That is, we knew about the symposium, of course. But not if we'd have any extra time afterward. But the sessions ended earlier today than we'd anticipated."

"I see." Sabrina saw that had the symposium ended later rather than sooner, they wouldn't have stopped by to see her at all.

"We thought we'd take a chance and see if you were home," her mother added.

"I'm home." It was a redundant statement, but she felt awkward.

"You're looking well," her mother said.

"Thanks. You are, too." Both her parents were tanned and healthy looking. They also looked stiffly ill at ease. "Why don't you both sit down. Would you like something to drink?"

"Some herbal tea would be nice," her mother said.

"How about you, Dad?"

"Nothing for me. I'm fine."

Meanwhile Brad had had it with hiding out in the bedroom like some kind of gigolo. He strolled into the living room as if he owned the place. "Hi there. I'm Brad Romanovski." He held out his hand to her father, who looked as if he didn't know what to do with it. After a brief pause, he shook Brad's hand firmly. Brad was surprised at how cold the other man's hand was. "You must be Sabrina's parents. Nice to meet you both. Martin and Leona, right?" He got that much from the symposium name tags they both still had attached to their matching safari jacket pockets. "Sabrina's told me a lot about you."

"Really?" Martin Stewart looked as if he couldn't imagine why his daughter would do that. "You mean she's told you about our work, correct?"

"Yes." Brad was mentally preparing himself for the inevitable question of what he was doing in their daughter's apartment at this time on a Sunday morning, coming from what was obviously the bedroom, with his hair disheveled and a shadowy jaw revealing the fact that he hadn't shaved since last night.

Instead Martin asked, "You're interested in the environment?"

Relieved at the reprieve, Brad replied, "I love the ocean."

"That's wonderful. Are you a marine biologist?"

"No. Just an interested citizen."

"In that case, we have some material we can give you about the terrible state our planet's oceans are in. Are you involved with Greenpeace or The Oceanic Society?"

"No."

"The Coastal Society?"

"Afraid not."

"You should really get in touch with those groups. They need all the support they can get." Martin and Leona Stewart spent the next hour talking to Brad in great detail about water-pollution problems from Peru to New Jersey.

The tea Sabrina had fixed for her mother sat untouched on the coffee table as Sabrina made herself comfortable on the rocking chair. Her mother might not need the soothing qualities of chamomile tea, but she sure did. She still couldn't believe her parents were here in her living room. This was their first visit to her apartment, but they'd made no mention of their surroundings—no comments on how nicely she'd done up the place or how lovely Violet's watercolor of the ocean looked on the wall over her dining room table.

But then Sabrina didn't expect anything else from her parents. They'd auctioned off most of their own belongings years ago. Possessions weren't important to them any longer and neither were people. The planet was. Sabrina was resigned to the realities of her parents' priorities.

Realizing Sabrina was being completely left out of the conversation, Brad attempted to include her. In his mind her parents' single-minded focus on the environment was similar to his grandfather's single-minded focus on the Cubs. The Stewarts were turning out to be much better than he'd expected. This he could handle, no problem.

"So," he said amiably, "how long has it been since you all have gotten together this way?"

"It's been a while. I'm not sure... might have been that oceanographic conference in Boston a few years back," her father noted. "Excellent conference."

"And how long are you going to be in town?" Brad asked, determined to keep the subject off the ocean for a while.

"Only a day or two."

"You know, Sabrina and I are going to a get-together at my grandparents' house this evening. Why don't you two come along? My family would love to meet you."

No, they wouldn't, Sabrina thought to herself. She'd seen what her parents could do to even the most enthusiastic and outgoing crowd. If they weren't discussing the environment, they couldn't hold a conversation for beans. Far safer to take them to a restaurant somewhere for dinner, or even have it here at her place.

But before she could voice either of those two options, Brad played the trump card. "My family would love to hear you talk about the environment."

Sabrina silently groaned, knowing that her parents would never turn down the opportunity to enlighten a new group of people as to the perils of plastic and pollution. There was nothing she could do now... except hope for the best and expect the worst.

When her parents returned to their friend's house to change clothes, Sabrina and Brad were left alone once again.

"Don't you think you should have asked your grandparents before inviting more guests over to their house?" Sabrina pointed out.

"You know my grandparents. The more, the merrier."

Merry? With her parents there? Unlikely. "Then you should have asked me."

"I already asked you if you wanted to go," Brad reminded her. "Several days ago. And you said yes."

"I meant that you should have asked me about asking my parents."

"This is getting too complicated here. If you've got a problem, just tell me what it is."

It would take at least an hour for her to verbalize the problem. How could she explain that seeing her parents again so unexpectedly this way had thrown her for a loop? The small things had hit her—like the way her parents never looked anyone straight in the eye for longer than four seconds. She'd timed it. She'd taken enough college psychology classes to know that it was a way of disengaging from the conversation, and from the other people in the conversation. Her parents were good at disengaging. She'd forgotten just *how* good. The realization brought back a lot of her doubts.

"You worry too much," Brad blithely informed her. Dropping a quick kiss on her mouth, he said, "Relax. Everything will be fine. I'll call my grandparents and work it all out."

When he returned to pick her up later that evening, Sabrina was no more optimistic than she had been when he'd left. She was running a bit late, so he followed her into her bedroom as she put on a few finishing touches to her outfit—including the earrings he'd given her.

"Doesn't that hurt?" he asked as she fastened the post through her earlobe.

"No." She met his eyes in the mirror. "You know, with your rebellious nature I half expected you to have a pierced earring of your own. A lot of men are wearing them now."

"Not me. No way." He picked up her perfume stopper and stroked it across the base of her throat. "I'm not that kind of guy."

"Astute kind of guys don't have pierced ears?"

"They'd rather nibble on their woman's ear," he murmured, making good on his words. "Great perfume."

"Thanks." She didn't melt against him as she usually did, though.

Brad noticed the difference. "You really are nervous about tonight, aren't you?"

"Yes." She stepped away from him and slipped into her shoes. "I told you, I don't think this is a very good idea. Your family is—"

"Warm and outgoing," Brad supplied.

"While my parents are—"

"Cold and distant. Would you just relax? It'll work out fine, you'll see. My family is so outgoing, they'll make up for your parents being quiet."

"You don't understand. My parents only have one interest. The environment. Talk about anything else and they're lost."

"Come on, don't you think you're exaggerating things a little here? They've done a lot of traveling, my family's always wanted to travel—that's a topic right there. We share an interest in the ocean, that's a second interest. You worry too much."

But when they walked in and found the room utterly quiet, Brad wondered if he'd worried too *little*. Her parents had gotten there before them—apparently having had no trouble with the map he'd drawn for them. His normally loquacious grandfather was rocking in his recliner with a choppy speed that reminded him of Sabrina's cat swishing its tail when it was aggravated. His grandmother was apparently hiding in the kitchen with his sister, while his parents were dutifully sitting on the couch, staring at their laps.

His family looked delighted to see him and Sabrina, indeed they latched on to their appearance with the eagerness of a drowning man grabbing a life preserver. Sabrina's parents barely looked mildly interested, however.

"Ah, there you are," Joseph said. "We were wondering what happened to you."

"Sorry we're late," Brad apologized.

"Well you're here now, that's all that matters. Glad you left your Mets cap at home tonight. My grandson only has one fault," Joseph told the Stewarts, "and that's liking the Mets instead of the Cubs. I'm a Cubs fan, myself," Joseph added.

Sabrina's parents smiled distantly but made no comment. At least Brad thought they smiled. He couldn't be sure if the slight lifting of their mouths was actually a smile or not. Their attitude was certainly livelier when they were talking about deforestation or water pollution, he noted.

"Sabrina's parents are environmentalists," Brad said.

"So I've heard. Do you know how long it takes a cigarette butt to disintegrate?" Joseph asked the Stewarts, obviously eager to show off his recently learned knowledge.

"Thirty years," Leona Stewart blandly replied.

"Only if it's in sunlight," Martin Stewart added.

"How about how long it takes for a glass bottle to disintegrate?" Joseph persisted.

"A million years," Martin replied. "And Americans toss out 811 million pounds of garbage every day. There are a lot of statistics we can tell you."

Joseph glared, clearly unhappy about someone else knowing more statistics than he did. He quickly changed the subject. "Did Sabrina tell you how she met our grandson? They knew each other as teenagers and then Brad hired her to make a family-chronicle video for our fiftieth anniversary."

"We're hoping Sabrina will give up that work and do something meaningful," Martin stated.

So much for that line of conversation, Brad reflected. He would have come to Sabrina's defense and said something, but she squeezed his arm and whispered, "Don't. It won't make any difference."

"But getting back to waste and recycling," Martin said. "I wonder if the public realizes how serious this problem is."

"You know something I've always wondered," Joseph inserted. "Why is it that people drop a letter in the mailbox and then open the lid again to make sure it really went down?"

Sabrina could see her parents looking at Joseph as if he were some strange specimen, an alien life form—which to them, he probably was.

"Haven't you ever done that?" Joseph asked.

Sabrina knew she'd done it a few times herself. The idea had obviously never occurred to her parents.

"Food's on," Violet announced.

The Romanovski family headed for the table as if they were being chased by wolves.

"At least you're using disposable plates," Leona noted. She held up a paper plate and studied it. "Are these made out of recycled paper?"

"I told you we should have used the good china!" a clearly upset Violet told Joseph.

"This is fine," Sabrina said with a warning glare in her mother's direction.

The conversation faltered after that as everyone took their plates and retired to their own corner of the room. While Sabrina paused to speak to Violet, Helen took the opportunity to needle Brad.

"Great party," she noted mockingly. "I don't think I've ever seen anyone dry up conversation faster than those two. Poor Sabrina."

Poor Sabrina, indeed, Brad agreed. He could kick himself for ever having suggested this get-together in the first place. What a mistake. Sabrina's parents' behavior this evening had opened his eyes. It certainly couldn't be having a very good effect on Sabrina herself.

Now that he'd spent time with the Stewarts, he could understand Sabrina's fears about her ability to love someone. Growing up with these two around was bound to make you doubt yourself. His main fear now was that their sudden appearance and aloof behavior this evening would only serve to strengthen Sabrina's doubts, undoing all the good he'd done in trying to build up her confidence.

Brad was determined not to let that happen.

The Stewarts left the party early, for which Brad was infinitely grateful. He hustled Sabrina out shortly thereafter. Instead of heading straight back to her place, he drove to one of his favorite spots overlooking the ocean.

All the while, Brad was plotting his strategy. Sabrina had been unusually quiet. He suspected she was already starting to doubt herself again...and her capacity to love. She'd tell him they were too different and haul out all the reasons why it wouldn't work out.

Brad planned on nipping those protests right in the bud. He'd start all over again if he had to—although he preferred the option of just kissing some sense into her—but he wasn't letting her go. No way.

As soon as he stopped the Corvette, he turned to her and said, "I think we need to clear up a few things here."

Sabrina looked at him uncertainly. Was Brad having second thoughts about their relationship? Had her parents driven him off, or simply driven him crazy? "What kind of things?" she asked hesitantly.

"First off, we've never talked about that fight we had over that piece of slime."

Sabrina looked at Brad in surprise. This was the last thing she'd expected him to bring up. "You want to talk about Guy?"

"No," he admitted honestly. Given a choice, he'd rather have dental work done than talk about Smut-Jones.

"Neither do I."

"Good. Then we'll consider the subject off limits from now on. The jerk left for Europe anyway."

"So Eliot told me."

"I see some other guy manhandling or threatening you, there's no guarantee I won't deck him, too," Brad felt obliged to warn her. "I'm no lapdog."

"No, you're not," Sabrina agreed. "You're more like a tomcat."

"Are you going to bring me in from the cold the way you did Thomas?" he inquired softly.

"It's more likely that *you've* brought *me* in from the cold," she murmured in reply. "You know, when my parents first arrived at my place and I saw how cold and distant they are, all those fears of mine came rushing back. So did the uncertainty. And when you seemed to get along with them so well, I began wondering if it was just me. Maybe *I* was the one who couldn't relate. But then I thought about it. I remembered the things you've told me. You've made me see myself in a new light, made me believe in myself. So I looked at the facts again and I realized that I relate to your family just fine. Walking into your grandparents' house is like walking into a hug. Or usually it feels that way. Tonight was the exception."

"Your parents do have a way of putting a damper on things."

"Yes, they do," she said. "Seeing them at your grandparents' tonight really opened my eyes. I don't interact with people the way my parents do. Not at all."

"That's for sure!" Brad heartily agreed before casually adding, "Think your father will give me any grief over wanting to marry his daughter?"

"Probably," Sabrina replied with an unsteady smile, her heart feeling about ready to burst. "He's given lots of people grief over the years. So has my mother. But you know what? They're not going to give me any more grief. Because I'm not like either of my parents. You taught me that. I *do* know how to love."

"Of course you do."

His I-told-you-so attitude made her laugh. She kissed him. "You know what made me see the light?"

"Me?"

"Yes, you. You made me look at things—at my parents and at myself—with new eyes. I realize now that I loved my parents when I was growing up, that's why their indifference hurt me so much. Apparently I had the ability to love all along and just didn't know it. Until you came along." She cupped his cheek with her hand, smiling as he turned to kiss the heart of her palm. "I can't change what's happened in the past, but I can prevent it from messing up my future." Sabrina took a deep breath before announcing, "I love you, Brad." She repeated it, louder this time. "I love you!"

"Then marry me," Brad said.

"You're sure?"

"Positive." His rough voice was very emphatic.

"It's a big step." She wanted to give him every opportunity to realize what he was getting into here. "Maybe you should think about it some more. After all, marrying me would make my parents your in-laws."

"Just answer the question."

"Yes," she said.

"Good. I can't wait to teach my new wife how to sail."

"How to sail...!" Before she could voice any further objections, Brad kissed her, and Sabrina forgot all about her aversion to choppy water. She forgot everything—except the man she loved.

* * * * *

COMING NEXT MONTH

#667 WILD ABOUT HARRY—Linda Lael Miller
Widowed mom Amy Ryan was sure she wasn't ready to love again. But why was she simply wild about Australia's *Man of the World*, Harry Griffith?

#668 A FINE MADNESS—Kathleen Korbel
It seemed someone thought that England's *Man of the World*, Matthew Spears, and Quinn Rutledge belonged together! Could they survive an eccentric ghost's matchmaking antics and discover romance on their own?

#669 ON HIS HONOR—Lucy Gordon
When Italy's *Man of the World*, Carlo Valetti, walked back into Serena Fletcher's life, she was nervous. Was this sexy charmer there to claim *her* love—or *his* daughter?

#670 LION OF THE DESERT—Barbara Faith
Morocco's *Man of the World*, Sheik Kadim al-Raji, had a mission—to rescue Diane St. James from kidnappers. But once they were safe, would this primitive male be able to let her go?

#671 FALCONER—Jennifer Greene
Shy Leigh Merrick knew life was no fairy tale, but then she met Austria's *Man of the World*, roguish Rand Krieger. This lord of the castle sent her heart soaring....

#672 SLADE'S WOMAN—BJ James
Fragile Beth Warren never dreamed she'd ever meet anyone like America's *Man of the World*, Hunter Slade. But this solitary man just wanted to be left alone....

AVAILABLE NOW:

#661 PRIDE AND JOY
Joyce Thies

#662 OUT OF DANGER
Beverly Barton

#663 THE MIDAS TOUCH
Cathryn Clare

#664 MUSTANG VALLEY
Jackie Merritt

#665 SMOOTH SAILING
Cathie Linz

#666 LONE WOLF
Annette Broadrick

SIX WILDLY SEXY HEROES FROM SIX SENSATIONAL COUNTRIES
MAN OF THE WORLD
ONLY IN

SILHOUETTE Desire

Have you ever longed to visit another country and meet your own special hero? Or maybe you think happiness can be found in your own backyard. No matter what, MAN OF THE WORLD is sure to fulfill your deepest desires. From Europe to the U.S.A., from Australia to the hot desert sands, when you open the covers of a MAN OF THE WORLD book, you'll find the man of your dreams waiting for you.

Travel to...

Australia in Linda Lael Miller's WILD ABOUT HARRY
England in Kathleen Korbel's A FINE MADNESS
Italy in Lucy Gordon's ON HIS HONOR
The kingdom of Rashdani in Barbara Faith's
  LION OF THE DESERT
Austria in Jennifer Greene's FALCONER
The United States in BJ James's SLADE'S WOMAN

MAN OF THE WORLD... available in October,
only in Silhouette Desire!

SDMOW